THE WICKED
WATERPARK
OF
WYOMING

Here's what readers from around the country are saying about Johnathan Rand's AMERICAN CHILLERS:

"Hey! I've read a lot of your boos and I really liked WASH-INGTON WAX MUSEUM. It was the best!"
-Olivia F., age 10, Michigan

"I'm your biggest fan! I read all of your books! Can you write a book and put my name in it?"
-Antonio D.,age 11, Florida

"We drove from Missouri to Michigan just to visit Chillermania!" It's the coolest book store in the world!
-Katelyn H., age 12, Missouri

"Thanks for writing such awesome books! I own every single American Chiller, but I can't decide which one I like best."
-Caleb C., Age 10, New Mexico

"Johnathan Rand is my favorite author in the whole world! Why does he wear those freaky glasses?"
-Sarah G., age 8, Montana

"I read all of your books, but the scariest book was TERRI-FYING TOYS OF TENNESSEE, because I live in Tennes-see and I am kind of scared of toys."
-Ana E., age 10, Tennessee

"I've read all of your books, and they're great! I'm reading CURSE OF THE CONNECTICUT COYOTES and it's AWESOME! Can you write about my town of Vashti, Texas?"

-Corey W., age 11, Texas

"I went to Chillermania on Saturday, April 29th, 2013. I love the store! I got the book THE UNDERGROUND UNDEAD OF UTAH and a MONSTER MOSQUITOES OF MAINE poster and a magic wand. I really want those sunglasses!"

-Justin S., age 9, Michigan

"You are the best author in the universe! I am obsessed with American and Michigan Chillers!"

-Emily N., age 10, Florida

"Last week I got into trouble for reading IDAHO ICE BEAST because I was supposed to be sleeping but I was in bed reading with a flashlight under the covers."

-Todd R., Minnesota

"At school, we had an American Chillers week, and all of the classes decorated the doors to look like an American Chillers book. Our class decorated our door to look like MISSISSIPPI MEGALODON and we won first place! We all got free American Chillers books! It was so cool!"

-Abby T., age 11, Ohio

"When school first started, I read FLORIDA FOG PHANTOMS. Then I got hooked on the series. I love your books!"

-Addison H, age 10, Indiana

"I just finished reading OKLAHOMA OUTBREAK. It was so scary that I thought there was a zombie behind me."

-Brandon C., Florida

"American Chillers books are AWESOME! I read them all the time!"

-Emilio S., age 11, Illinois

"Your books are great! Me and my friend started our own series. Your books should become a TV series. That would be cool!"

-Camerron S., age 9, Delaware

"In first grade, I read Freddie Fernortner, Fearless First Grader. Now I'm reading the American Chillers series, and I love them! My favorite is OREGON OCEANAUTS, because it has a lot of adventure and suspense."

-Megan G., age 12, Arkansas

Got something cool to say about Johnathan Rand's books? Let us know, and we might publish it right here! Send your short blurb to:

Chiller Blurbs
281 Cool Blurbs Ave.
Topinabee, MI 49791

Other books by Johnathan Rand:

AMERICA'S #1 SERIES FOR MAXIMUM CHILLS!

#38: The Wicked Waterpark of Wyoming

Johnathan Rand

An AudioCraft Publishing, Inc. book

Book storage and warehouses provided by Chillermania!©
Indian River, Michigan

American Chillers #38: The Wicked Waterpark of Wyoming
ISBN 13-digit: 978-1-893699-52-6

Librarians/Media Specialists:
PCIP/MARC records available **free of charge** at
www.americanchillers.com

Cover illustration by Dwayne Harris
Cover layout and design by Sue Harring

Printed in USA

The
Wicked
Waterpark
of
Wyoming

VISIT CHILLERMANIA!

WORLD HEADQUARTERS FOR BOOKS BY JOHNATHAN RAND!

CHILLERMANIA!

**I-75 Exit 313
then south
1 mile!**

Visit the HOME for books by Johnathan Rand! Featuring books, hats, shirts, bookmarks and other cool stuff not available anywhere else in the world! Plus, watch the American Chillers website for news of special events and signings at *CHILLERMANIA!* with author Johnathan Rand! Located in northern lower Michigan, on I-75! Take exit 313 . . . then south 1 mile! For more info, call (231) 238-0338. And be afraid! Be veeeery afraaaaaaiiiid . . . .

My name is Madison Armstrong, and when people find out that I'm afraid of waterparks, they look at me kind of funny. They wonder if I'm afraid of the water, or they might wonder if I can swim. No, I'm not afraid of the water, and I'm an excellent swimmer. In fact, I've been swimming for longer than I can even remember. My mom says that I was swimming when I was only two years old.

So, no, water doesn't scare me, and I'm a great swimmer.

But waterparks? Well, that's a completely different story. It's also a horrifying story, and it really happened to me and my friend, Griffin

Claremont. But to fully understand the horror we went through, you need to know how we got to the waterpark, and why we were there in the first place.

Actually, when I think about it, we went to the waterpark for the same reason most families go to waterparks: a vacation. It's a time for Mom and Dad to get away from work and not think about too many things. And it's a time for kids like me to do something different, meet new friends, splash around, and have a great time.

But it was my older brother, Sam, who found out about the waterpark. Sam is fifteen, and he thinks he knows *everything*. We used to hang out together a lot, but now he has other friends he spends his time with. I'm twelve, and he says he doesn't want to hang out with a "little girl." Which I don't think is fair, but I don't really mind. I have a lot of friends of my own. And besides: Sam and I really don't get into arguments or fights like a lot of other brothers and sisters do.

"Check this out, Chicky-Poo," Sam said.

Chicky-Poo is a nickname he'd just started calling me. I didn't really like it, but I could think of a lot worse names he could call me.

"What?" I asked.

He'd just walked into the house and was carrying a piece of mail. It was a colorful brochure addressed to the Armstrong Family.

"There's a new waterpark opening near Casper," he said, handing me the brochure. Casper is about two and a half hours northwest of where we live in Cheyenne, Wyoming. I'd never been to Casper before, but Mom and Dad had gotten married there and lived there before Sam and I were born.

I looked at the brochure filled with pictures of smiling, happy people, splashing in pools and plummeting down steep slides. The brochure stated that the new waterpark, called WonderSplash, was state-of-the art and would be opening in July, one month from now.

And while WonderSplash looked like a lot of fun, I didn't think too much of it at the time.

Casper was over two hours away, and the waterpark would be opening right in the middle of summer. Usually, our family takes vacations in the winter, and we go somewhere warm like southern California or Texas.

So, after I'd glanced over the brochure, I almost threw it in the waste basket.

Almost.

Instead, the phone rang, and I went to answer it. I put the brochure on the kitchen counter as I chatted on the phone with a friend from school. She told me all about her new kitten, about how cute he was, and that she was going to email me some pictures later in the day.

And I forgot all about the WonderSplash brochure that I'd placed on the counter.

Now, looking back, I wonder if things would have been different if the phone hadn't rang. Probably. I probably wouldn't have been distracted and would have thrown away the WonderSplash brochure. That way, Dad wouldn't have found it. He wouldn't have thought that a short, midsummer vacation to the waterpark would be great fun.

No, if the phone hadn't rang, if I'd thrown away the WonderSplash brochure and Dad had never seen it, I wouldn't have wound up with the starring role in the most horrifying nightmare I'd ever experienced.

One month later:

"There it is, up ahead."

Mom's words woke me from a sound sleep in the backseat of our car. I didn't really remember drifting off. I remembered being sleepy, closing my eyes, and resting my head on the seat. I remembered the constant, monotonous drone of the highway beneath our tires making me sleepy.

When I heard Mom's voice and opened my eyes, I knew I must've been asleep for at least an hour. While it wasn't quite dark yet, the sun had dipped beneath the trees and the shadows were long.

And ahead of us, in twilight's murky gloom, WonderSplash rose into the darkening sky. A tangle of thick, dark green tubes climbed into the air, twisting and turning, reflecting a hint of moonlight that was beginning to bloom as the sun fell farther and farther into the horizon.

And to my surprise, my brother spoke, and he had the same thought that was on *my* mind.

"That looks creepy," he said. "It doesn't look like a place where families go to have fun."

"That's because all of the lights are off," Dad said. "You saw the brochure. It'll look a lot different in the daytime. The weather is supposed to be perfect, and I think we're all going to have a great time."

I rubbed the sleep from my eyes with the palms of my hands. "That thing looks like it's alive," I said. "It looks like a monster of some sort."

"That's all in the design," Dad said. "It's supposed to look that way, to attract attention."

Dad pulled to the side of the road and stopped. The parking lot in front of WonderSplash was enormous, and cones of white light hung in the air from tall light posts, illuminating a few colorful vans. The vans were identical and depicted scenes from WonderSplash. The words *Courtesy Shuttle* were on the sides of each vehicle.

And beyond the parking lot, the dark waterpark loomed like a silent, monstrous octopus, a sleeping beast waiting to wake, to rise, to pounce on tiny, helpless victims, to swallow them whole, so they would never be seen again. In the shadows, I could even make out what appeared to be eyes and claws.

"Now that I think about it, we're going to have a blast," my brother said. "This place looks awesome. Creepy, but awesome."

I hoped my brother was right, but I had my doubts. I'd never had such a helpless feeling of despair in my life. I tried to tell myself that it was just my imagination, that I was just being silly, but it was no use. I just couldn't shake the fear that was growing inside me, swelling larger and larger, making me anxious and tense.

"You okay, Maddie?" my dad asked. I caught the shadowy reflection of his eyes gazing at me in the car's rearview mirror.

"Yeah," I said, managing a weak smile. "Just sleepy."

"We'll check into our hotel, and you can get a good night's sleep," Dad said. "The waterpark doesn't open until the day after tomorrow, but I'm glad we came a day early. Your mother and I haven't been back to Casper since before both of you were born."

The car slowly pulled away, and I looked again at the enormous waterpark, at the maze of slides and tubes and funnels that rose into the darkening sky.

Then, I *knew*.

I *knew* that something was really, really wrong with WonderSplash, but I had no idea what it was.

Nor did I know that in less than twenty-four

hours, I would be fighting an all-out war against unimaginable odds, in an all-out struggle just to stay alive.

3

The hotel was called WonderSplash Vacation Resort, and it was only about a mile farther down the road. It rose six stories into the night sky, and it was brightly lit. The parking lot was nearly full. Obviously, many families had done the same thing we had: arrived more than a full day early. The parking lot was filled with vehicles, and nearly every window on every floor of the hotel glowed behind closed curtains. Out front, between the parking lot and the big awning that covered the entrance to the lobby, a large fountain sat in the middle of a shallow pool, spewing water into the air. Spotlights on the ground were directed up, illuminating the sprays and creating millions of glittering, liquid diamonds that rose into an arc before falling into the rippling water.

Dad parked the car, and the four of us got out. We retrieved our suitcases from the trunk and began zigzagging our way around other parked cars, past the fountain, and beneath the awning to large, glass doors that automatically opened as we approached.

The inside of the hotel was clean, with creamy, marble floors that reflected the lights from above. In the lobby, a few tables and comfy chairs were placed all around, and there were two cozy couches and two plush recliners. A family had just finished checking in, and as they headed for their room, the man behind the desk looked up at us and smiled.

"Reservation?" he asked.

Dad and Mom approached the desk, while Sam and I marveled at the lobby. I'd stayed in only a couple of hotels before, but they were nothing like WonderSplash Vacation Resort. Maybe I was going to like our little vacation, after all.

Dad thanked the man behind the desk, and he and Mom approached us.

"Top floor, room 615," Dad said, and Sam and I followed our parents as they led us through the lobby, down a long, glistening hall, to the brushed-steel double doors of an elevator. In no time at all, we were in our room, unpacking our belongings.

The room was big. It had two separate bedrooms, two bathrooms, and a kitchen with a stove, refrigerator, and microwave. There was a large, flat screen television on a dark desk, and there were televisions in each bedroom.

"Maddie," Dad said as he plucked a gallon-sized plastic bucket from the counter. "Can you run down the hall and get some ice? The machine is past the elevator on the left."

"Yeah," I said, taking the bucket from him.

"Here," Mom said, handing me a plastic card

that served as our room key. "You'll need this to get back in."

I stuffed the card into my pocket and left. The hall was empty, and my shoes whispered on the soft, red carpet as I made my way past doors on either side of me. In some rooms, I could hear the tinny sounds of televisions; in others, I heard muffled, boisterous laughter.

Ahead, just past the elevator, a sign stuck out from the wall: *Ice/Vending*.

When I reached the entryway to the small room, I turned, facing two machines. One contained several flavors of soft drinks and bottled water, and the other was filled with assorted candy bars and snacks. On the far wall was an ice machine. I approached it, holding the bucket out, reaching for the button . . . unaware that someone was waiting for me, tucked in the shadows of the two machines. Before I even had a chance to place the bucket beneath the ice dispenser, powerful arms had wrapped around my neck, dragging me to the floor!

I screamed. At the same time, I dropped the plastic bucket and drove my right elbow backward in an attempt to break free. My elbow met soft flesh, and I heard a grunt as the arms around my neck released me. I leapt up and spun to see a boy of about my age on the floor, grasping his stomach with both hands. His eyes were wide and filled with surprise, and he was doubled over in pain.

"You're . . . you're not my sister!" he wheezed, gasping for breath.

"No, I'm not," I said. Now that I knew I

wasn't in danger, my blood boiled. "What did you do *that* for?"

"I . . . was only trying to get back at my sister for scaring me earlier today," he said. "I'm really sorry. My . . . my sister said she was coming down here to buy a candy bar. While she went down to the lobby to get change, I snuck in here and hid between the machines. I thought you were Abbie. I . . . I thought you were my sister."

It began to make sense. He wasn't trying to hurt or scare me. He was only trying to get back at his sister for scaring him. I felt bad that I had hit him so hard in the stomach, but I really *had* thought I was in serious danger.

"I'm sorry for hitting you," I said. "Can you stand up?"

The boy rolled to his knees. Placing one hand on the side of the ice machine, he stood.

"Wow," he said as he rubbed his stomach. "I don't know who you are, but remind me never to make you really mad."

"I'm Madison," I said. "Madison Armstrong.

28

My family is here for the opening of the waterpark."

"Mine, too," the boy replied. "Although, I think it would've been a better idea if we would've left my sister at home. She drives me crazy."

"My brother drives me crazy sometimes," I said. "He's only a couple of years older than me, and he thinks he knows everything."

"I'm Griffin Claremont," the boy said. "Did you guys just get here today?"

I nodded. "Just a few minutes ago," I said. "We just checked into our room."

"Isn't this place great?" Griffin said.

"It sure is," I said. "I've never stayed at a hotel this big before."

I knelt down and picked up the plastic ice bucket that had fallen to the floor.

"I'd better get some ice back to our room," I said. "Maybe I'll see you around the park?"

"Yeah," Griffin said. "Maybe. See you later."

Griffin left, and I filled the bucket with ice.

Back at our hotel room, I told Mom and Dad

what had happened.

"It sounds like you gave him quite a bit of a scare," Mom said.

"Nothing like the scare he gave me," I said.

Each bedroom had two large double beds, which meant that my parents would sleep in one room, and Sam and I would share the other. That wasn't a big deal, but my brother had started snoring within the last year. At our house, I could hear him snoring from his bedroom, and it was all the way down at the other end of the hall! Even Mom and Dad said his snoring was bad, and I made him close his bedroom door at night. I hoped he wouldn't be snoring in our hotel room, or none of us would get any sleep.

I needn't have worried. I fell into such a deep sleep that I don't think a freight train could have awakened me. I slept well, but I had bizarre nightmares about an enormous waterpark that was really a giant octopus that came alive. I awoke in the middle of the night with a start, realizing I had been dreaming, thankful that the experience had been only in my imagination.

If only things were to remain that way. If only the terror that I had felt earlier that night and during my nightmare had remained in my mind, only a part of my imagination.

But how was I to know? How was I to know that Griffin and I were about to get tangled up in a real-life situation that was worse than any nightmare?

The next morning, we had breakfast in the lobby, and the air was filled with the tantalizing smells of eggs, bacon, pancakes, and coffee. There were many families seated around the tables. Everyone was laughing and chatting, in a good mood, ready for the grand opening of the waterpark the next day.

"We're going to take a drive to see our old home," Mom said. "Then, we're going to drive around the city to see what's changed since we moved."

That did *not* seem like a lot of fun. It was a nice day, and I didn't want to spend it inside the car, driving around.

Sam was thinking the exact same thing. "You don't mind if I stay here, do you?" he asked. "Even though the waterpark isn't open, there are lots of things to do."

"Yeah," I agreed. "Can I stay, too?"

"You guys don't want to see where your mother and I used to live?" Dad asked.

I looked at my brother, and he looked at me. We both shook our heads, then looked at Dad.

"Not really," we both said in unison.

Dad shrugged. "That's fine," he said. "Just don't get into trouble."

An hour later, Sam and I were alone in our hotel room. Mom and Dad had left, saying they would be back sometime after lunch. Sam wasted no time, taking a seat in front of the television with the controls for the video game in his lap.

"Is that all you're going to do?" I asked. "Play video games all day?"

"Why not?" Sam replied.

"Because there are trails all over the place," I said. "And this hotel has a pool and a playground outside."

"I'll have enough time to swim at the waterpark over the next couple of days," Sam replied, his eyes fixed on the TV screen. "And I'm a little too old to be playing on the playground."

"Well, I'm going to go exploring," I said.

"Remember what Dad told you," Sam said. "Don't get into trouble."

I rode the elevator down to the lobby, where I found a huge rack of brochures. They were all different, each one advertising different forms of entertainment, from hot air balloon rides to restaurants, horseback riding, miniature golf, and even white water rafting.

"Hey, Madison," said a voice. I turned to see Griffin walking toward me.

I smiled. "How's your stomach?"

He rubbed his stomach with the palm of his hand. "I think I'll live," he said. "But the next time

I decide to try to scare my sister, I'm gonna make sure that it's actually her. Hey . . . do you want to go tour WonderSplash?"

I cocked my head and frowned. "Tour the waterpark?" I said. "But it doesn't open until tomorrow."

"It doesn't," Griffin said. "But they're giving free tours of the park today, before it actually opens. I thought it would be fun to check it out."

That *did* seem like it would be fun. We'd be able to get a look at the waterpark before most other kids, kind of a 'behind-the-scenes' sneak preview. A tour might be pretty cool.

"Come on," Griffin said. "I was just about to catch one of the shuttles."

"Hang on a minute," I said. "I need to tell my brother where I'm going."

Griffin pointed to a phone on the wall. "Use that phone," he said. "Just dial your hotel room number."

I did as Griffin instructed. My brother answered, but he was distracted by his video game. I told him about the tour and that Griffin and I were going to check out WonderSplash.

"Don't get into trouble," he warned, once again echoing Dad's words.

I hung up.

"Let's go!" I said to Griffin. "This is going to be cool!"

In the parking lot, we boarded one of the shuttle vans I'd seen the night before. Griffin and I were the only passengers.

"Looks like it's just you two on this trip," the driver said as he closed the door.

"You mean that we're the only people getting a tour of the waterpark?" Griffin asked.

The driver laughed. "Oh, no," he said. "We've been driving people back and forth all morning already. It's just that you are the only two riding in the van on this trip."

The shuttle van pulled out of the parking lot and turned onto the main road, heading for WonderSplash.

"You know," I said to Griffin, "when I saw

the waterpark for the first time last night, I was a little freaked out."

Griffin frowned. "Why?"

"I'm not really sure," I answered. "Maybe because it was all dark and shadowy and looked like a giant creature."

"I think it's supposed to," Griffin said.

"I'm sure it will look a lot more fun in the daytime," I said. "And I think this tour will be interesting."

In minutes, the shuttle van was approaching the waterpark. I could see the huge, green pipes twisting and turning beneath the blue sky. I tried to imagine what it was going to be like sliding through them, splashing down into the pool at the bottom.

The van began to slow . . . and then disaster struck. There was a sudden explosion that sounded like a shotgun going off—and suddenly the van spun wildly out of control!

Griffin and I were knocked to the floor.

"Hang on!" the driver yelled as the van lurched to one side, its tires screeching and squealing. For a moment, I thought we were going to flip over, but the van stopped and came to rest on all four wheels.

"You kids okay?" the driver asked.

"I am," I replied.

"Me, too," Griffin said. "What happened?"

"Blew a tire, I think," the driver said. "Never had that happen before. Must've run over something. You sure you guys are okay?"

Griffin got to his feet, and he helped me up.

"Yeah," I said. "We're fine."

"Might as well just let you off here," the driver said, "being that we're only a few hundred yards from the waterpark."

"Do you need any help?" I asked, which was kind of silly, as I didn't know anything about changing a tire, and I doubted Griffin did, either.

"No, thanks," the driver said. "I'll just radio back to the hotel and let them know what happened. I can probably replace the tire with the spare in the back."

He opened the door and let us out.

"Bye," I said, and the man waved and smiled.

"Have fun on the tour," he said, and he picked up the radio's microphone.

"That was freaky," Griffin said. "That blown tire was loud."

"He probably ran over a nail or something," I said.

It took us only about a minute to walk to the waterpark. There were more cars in the lot than what we'd seen the night before, and one of the other colorful shuttle buses had just dropped off some people and was pulling out of the parking lot.

"Where do we go?" Griffin asked.

I pointed. "Over there, I think," I said. "That's where everyone else seems to be going. Let's follow them."

We walked across the parking lot and found a wide, tunnel-like entrance with a big welcome sign above it. Several people had just vanished within the tunnel. Above us, the dark green tubes loomed large beneath a perfect blue sky.

"You said the tour doesn't cost anything?" I asked.

Griffin shook his head. "A guy back at the hotel said that it's free. Of course, we don't get to go on any slides or rides or anything. It's just a tour to show the inner workings of WonderSplash. Still, I think it will be fun."

"Me, too," I said. "I've never been to a waterpark before. It'll be fun to find out how they work."

The entrance doors were open, and we joined a crowd of people waiting in the main lobby. Soon, the crowd began walking forward into a hallway and through a narrow set of open double doors. Griffin and I followed.

Suddenly, we were stopped by a man who was standing by the doors. He was wearing dark blue pants and a light blue shirt with the colorful WonderSplash logo across the chest. The doors swung shut behind the group of people.

"Hang on just a few minutes for the next tour," the man said, smiling. "We allow only twenty-five people at a time on the tour. It'll just be a few minutes before the next tour starts." Then, the man looked at his watch. "I'll be right back," he said.

We were alone in the large lobby. There were several banks of cash registers on desks, but those areas were roped off.

"Tomorrow, this place is going to be packed," Griffin said.

"I can't wait," I said, trying to forget the dread and unease I'd felt the night before. By now, I was certain it had all been my imagination. Waterparks were happy places, places for fun and laughter, places to smile and splash and have the time of your life.

"I'm going to see if I can find a restroom," Griffin said, looking around.

I peered down an unlit hallway on the other side of the lobby.

"There might be one down there," I said, pointing.

"I'll go check," said Griffin.

"I'll wait right here," I said.

Griffin hustled off, and I watched him as he made his way down the shadowy hall. I liked him. He was nice and seemed like a lot of fun.

"I don't see any light switches," Griffin said as he made his way down the murky hall. "Sure is dark."

Then, he vanished in the gloom.

"Be careful," I called out.

"Don't worry," Griffin called back. "I think there's a door here."

I heard a clicking sound, metal on metal, like a door opening.

"Wow," he said. "This door is hard to open. I'm not sure if—"

Griffin's voice was abruptly cut off by the sound of a slamming door. Then, all I could hear was a muffled scream, as if he was falling. In seconds, his wails had faded, and I knew something awful had happened to him.

But I didn't know something awful was about to happen to me, too.

I suppose it would've been better if I hadn't gone to help Griffin. Who knows what would've happened if I had waited for the man to return. Then, I could have told him something happened to Griffin, and we never would have wound up in such a mess.

But Griffin was my friend, even though I'd known him only a few days. He was my friend, and I knew he was in trouble. I had to help him.

"Griffin!" I shouted.

I sprinted across the lobby and into the dark hall. Griffin had opened a door, and I needed to find it.

"Griffin?!?!" I called out again. "Can you hear me? Are you okay?"

I listened, but heard nothing. There were no sounds whatsoever.

"Griffin?" I called out again, my eyes scanning the hall.

Cautiously, I continued down the dark hall, feeling the wall with my hand, searching for a door.

There.

I felt the cold metal of a doorknob and gave it a twist. I tried pulling it open, but it was difficult, as if there was someone on the other side trying to keep it closed, pulling against me. For a second, I wondered if it was Griffin just playing a trick.

No, I thought. *No, he wasn't playing a trick. His screams were real.*

I tugged harder at the door, and it finally opened, but I wasn't prepared for what happened next.

It was as if I opened up the door of a

vacuum. A strong gust of air pulled at me, yanking me into darkness, causing me to stumble forward. I heard the door slam behind me and threw up my hands in front of me to break my fall on the floor.

But the floor never came. I had been prepared to hit it and get back up, but that's not what happened.

Instead, I found myself tumbling, falling, end over end in a free fall, spinning downward through the darkness!

All of the horror, all of the terror I'd felt the night before came rushing back. I remembered how I'd felt upon first seeing the giant, shadowy mountain of WonderSplash last night, and I realized that my gut feeling had been right. There was something inside of me that had tried to warn me away from the place. Somehow, my inner alarm had gone off, telling me that all was not right with the waterpark, that I'd better stay away.

But I hadn't listened to it. I had pushed the thoughts out of my mind, telling myself that I was being silly, that it was just an ordinary waterpark.

Now, I knew differently. I didn't know anything else, of course, but I was now certain that I was in a lot of trouble.

And so was Griffin.

It was with great relief that I suddenly found myself plunging feet-first into warm water. I went completely under before thrashing to the surface, gasping for air.

"Madison! Is that you?" I heard Griffin shout from nearby. His voice was booming and hollow, like we were in a large, empty room. But it was so dark, I couldn't see a thing.

"Wha . . . what's going on?" I sputtered.

"I don't know," Griffin replied. "But there's some sort of solid floor over here. Swim toward me."

"Keep talking so I know I'm heading in the right direction," I replied.

"Okay," he said, and he began telling me how he'd been pulled through the door, tumbled through the air, and landed in the water, and how he'd started swimming and bumped into something hard, like the edge of a pool. All the while, I listened to his voice and swam in his direction.

Soon, my hand hit something solid, and I stopped swimming.

"I'm right here," Griffin said, and his hand found my wrist. "Climb up."

With Griffin's help, I pulled myself out of the water and sat on a hard surface made of concrete or steel. My legs dangled in the water. Although I knew Griffin was only inches away, I couldn't see him.

"What just happened?" I asked again. "Where are we?"

"I don't know," Griffin answered, "but I'm glad to be alive. I'm glad we landed in water and not on cement or something else."

"What happened with that door?" I asked. "When I opened it, it was like a huge vacuum cleaner turned on. The suction pulled me in, and there wasn't anything I could do about it. "

"That's what happened to me," Griffin said. "The important thing is that neither one of us is hurt. Now we have to find a way out of here."

"We'll have to be careful," I said. "It's going to be nearly impossible to find a way out if we can't see where we're going."

Beside me, I could hear dripping water. Griffin, too, had been dangling his legs in the water, and he pulled them out and swung them to the side, bumping me in the process.

"Sorry," he said as I rolled sideways and stood. A lock of my wet hair fell into my face, and I pulled it away.

"Where's your hand?" Griffin asked. I held out my hand and slowly moved it around until I found Griffin.

"Hang on," he said. "We'll have to move carefully, so we don't run into any more surprises."

As soon as he said those words, both of us bumped into a surprise, but this time it was in the form of a wall. We were moving slowly, so we didn't get hurt.

I raised my free hand and felt a cool, hard surface.

"Let's follow the wall this way," Griffin said, and he slowly pulled me to the right, following the wall, both of us taking cautious baby steps so we wouldn't trip over anything or fall into the water again.

I was dragging my hand along the cool wall when my fingers touched something small. I stopped walking.

"Wait a minute," I said. "I think I found something."

I fumbled around for another moment, until I found what I was looking for. When I touched it again, I knew immediately what it was.

A light switch.

I flipped it up. An explosion of white illuminated our surroundings with harsh, bright light, and what we saw gave Griffin and me the shock of our lives . . . .

We were in a dome-shaped, round room. Above, in the center of the dome, was a large, dark hole, the place we'd fallen through. A narrow walkway went all the way around the edge of a large, deep pool, which was so deep that we couldn't even see the bottom, even in the bright, overhead lights mounted in the ceiling. On the opposite side from where we were, two dark corridors tunneled into blackness.

"Where are we?" Griffin whispered.

I shook my head, but I couldn't speak. I was

too amazed at what we were seeing. Although I had never been to a waterpark before, something told me that this wasn't normal, that most waterparks probably didn't have hidden pools beneath them.

It just didn't add up.

"Well, we know we're somewhere inside WonderSplash," I said. "There's a way in, so there must be a way out."

Griffin pointed to the hole at the top of the dome. "Let's hope that's not the only way in or out," he said. "Otherwise, we're going to be stuck here for a long, long time."

Griffin followed the narrow space of flooring that separated the wall and the pool. I fell in line behind him, and we stopped when we reached one of the hallways on the other side.

"See a light switch?" he asked, as we stared into the cavernous gloom.

I shook my head. "Nope," I said.

"Let's try the next one," Griffin said.

We didn't find any light switch near that

hall, either.

"Well," I said, placing my hands on my hips. "Maybe we'll just have to take our chances. These halls have to lead somewhere. There must be another way out."

Griffin stared into the dark hallway.

"Yeah, I guess you're right," he said. "We'll just have to go slowly and be careful."

We were about to step into the hallway, but were stopped by a distant sound. It was a scuffling noise, the sound of someone walking . . . sort of. It was coming from the darkness, deep in the hallway.

Griffin and I froze.

"Someone's coming!" I whispered.

"That's a relief," Griffin said. "Now we can get out of here."

I stepped to the side of the hall, pulling Griffin with me. While he was thinking that someone was coming who could help us, I was thinking something completely different. My inner alarm had gone off again, telling me that trouble was on its way. This time, I wasn't going to ignore it.

"What are you afraid of?" Griffin asked.

"I don't know," I said. "But something's not right."

"I could have told you that," he said. "We both got sucked through a doorway. We shouldn't even be here."

The sounds coming from the dark hallway were becoming louder. It sounded like lazy footsteps, like someone dragging their feet.

The only place to hide was in the other hallway, and I quickly walked to it and darted inside. Griffin followed, and we crouched down, peering around the corner.

"I'm sure it's just someone who works here," he whispered.

"Maybe so," I whispered back. *"But just in case."*

The sounds were louder now, and not only could we hear the sound of footsteps, but also a strange, slurping sound, like someone was licking their lips. I tucked tighter into the corner, and Griffin peered over my shoulder.

The noises stopped. I held my breath.

Then, we saw a flash of movement, and we knew instantly that what we were seeing most certainly wasn't an employee of the waterpark. Emerging from the hall was something that wasn't even human.

We were staring at a monster.

I covered my mouth to stifle a gasp. Every muscle in my body tightened. We could only watch as the hideous creature emerged from the hall and stood at the edge of the pool.

"What is that thing?" Griffin whispered.

"Shhhh!" I hissed back.

The creature was about my height, but he was dark green. He had a frog-like face, and his arms were long and muscular. His hands, however, were wide, like paddles, and he had three fingers with sharp talons at the ends. His legs were larger, even more muscular than his arms, and he had a tail that dragged behind him on the ground.

The slimy beast turned his head, and Griffin and I tucked deeper into the hall, deeper into the shadows so he couldn't see us. We heard a heavy splash, and I peeked around the corner just in time to see the thing vanish beneath the churning surface of the pool.

Neither of us moved nor spoke for nearly a minute. Finally, I stood, and Griffin did the same. I took a cautious step to the edge of the pool, searching the dark waters for any sign of the creature.

Nothing. The creature had vanished.

"Where do you think he went?" Griffin asked.

I shook my head. "I don't know, and I don't care," I said. "That was the freakiest creature I have ever seen in my life, and I hope I never see him again."

"Maybe going down the hallway isn't such a good idea, after all," Griffin said.

I looked around the dome-shaped room, at the hole in the ceiling, then back to the water, my eyes probing the murky depths.

"Well, we can't stay here," I said. "There might be more of those things. If there are, sooner or later, they're going to find us."

"What do you suppose it is?" Griffin asked.

I shrugged. "I don't know. Some half-lizard, half-frog creature."

"Let's try the other hallway," Griffin suggested.

"Six of one, half dozen of the other," I said.

"What?" Griffin asked.

"Oh, that's just a saying my mom always says. Six of one, half dozen of the other. It means that what choice you make really doesn't make any difference. You know: six of one, half dozen of the other."

"Oh," Griffin said. "I get it. It really doesn't matter which hallway we choose, because the odds are about the same."

"Right," I said. "But let's go down that one,"

I continued, pointing at the other hall.

Then, without warning, the water exploded only a few feet from us. There was no time to do anything, no time to flee, as the horrifying half-frog, half-lizard creature burst up from the dark waters, seized Griffin and me with his powerful arms, and dragged us down into the dark pool!

Now, I know what a lot of people are going to think. They're going to think that if they were in the same position Griffin and I were in, they would just jump out of the way or run off.

But no, they wouldn't.

Because if we would have had time, that's what *we* would have done. But we had no warning at all. We never saw the dark shadow shooting toward us from the depths of the pool. In less than two seconds, we were snared by the awful beast and pulled beneath the surface. We didn't even have time to scream, and there was no time to struggle. One moment we were standing on the walkway next to the pool, and in the next instant, we were under water.

I kicked and flailed my arms, lashing out with all my strength. Bubbles swirled around me, and I could feel myself being pulled deeper and deeper. Everything had happened so fast that I didn't have a chance to take a deep breath, and I knew that if I didn't get out of the clutches of the creature, I was going to run out of air.

But that might be the least of our worries. What if he was going to eat us? What if we were going to be his next meal?

Despite my struggling, I could feel his powerful arm holding me tight. It seemed easy for him to hold his grip on me, seemingly without any effort at all. Despite all of my kicking and punching and flailing around, my efforts were in vain.

Down, down we went, deeper and deeper, until darkness enveloped us. I could no longer see the bubbles whirling about, nor could I see the creature's powerful arm wrapped around my waist. The darkness took over, and my lungs ached. I needed to breathe, but I knew that if I opened my mouth, water would come pouring in.

I had one more chance. I mustered every bit of strength I had left in a last-ditch effort to break free from the clutches of the awful monstrosity that was holding me captive, pulling me deeper and deeper into the dark water.

Using both my arms and my legs, I pushed and twisted with every ounce of energy I had. For a moment, I thought I was going to break free, but the creature easily tightened his grip on me. When he did, he squeezed my stomach, forcing me to expel the air in my chest. My mouth was forced open, the last of my air went out . . . and water came pouring in.

My reflex after exhaling the last of my air was to inhale. I tried to close my mouth, I tried not to breathe in, but it was no use. Water rushed into my mouth and nostrils, burning my throat.

And I knew that this was it. There was to be no more struggle, no more hope. I was going to swallow water, and it would fill my lungs. I was going to drown, and that's all there was to it.

But that's not what happened at all.

Despite the sudden, automatic reflex causing me to breathe in through my mouth and nose, I found it wasn't necessary. I didn't swallow the water in my mouth, but instead, I spit it out. I no longer felt like I needed to breathe. It was as if I was continuing to hold my breath, even though I had no more breath to hold.

But maybe this is what drowning is like, I thought. *Maybe I'll pass out in another moment.*

Nope. I remained awake and aware as we plunged deeper and deeper, farther and farther through the inky waters. I stopped struggling, knowing that my efforts were useless. The only thing I could do was hope that my kidnapper, whatever sort of bizarre creature he was, wasn't going to have me as a late-morning snack.

And Dad told me not to do anything to get into trouble, I thought. *Hah. I'm in trouble, all right. I'm in more trouble than I could have possibly ever imagined.*

My surroundings began to lighten, and I could make out the fuzzy shape of the alien-like beast that held me in his clutches. Next to me, I could see the gauzy figure of Griffin, and I wondered if he was okay. Then, I saw him move his arm, and I knew he was alive.

But where were we going? Where was this thing taking us? I suddenly felt like I was starring in some crazy science fiction or fantasy movie.

Or maybe I wasn't the star, after all. In movies, the star always saves the day and lives. Maybe Griffin and I weren't going to be so lucky.

Strangest of all, I still didn't feel the need to breathe.

I could feel us slowing down. Our surroundings became brighter and brighter, and then I realized there was some sort of light below us. But I couldn't see it very well, because it was blurry under water. Whenever I went swimming in a lake or stream and opened my eyes under water, everything was blurry. I read in my science book at school that it was because air and water are affected differently by light. When water comes in contact with the eye, it causes the eye to focus differently, because our eyes are made to focus on light that travels through air. Which, the book explained, was why you can see perfectly fine under water with a mask or goggles.

I squinted, trying to see better under the water, but it didn't work very well. Everything was still very blurry. But I could tell that we had reached the bottom, as I could make out what appeared to be rocks, sand, and even seaweed.

Even stranger, I thought. I had thought we were in some sort of pool, but that's not what this was at all. We seemed to be in some sort of underground lake or pond.

The creature was still holding onto us as tightly as ever. He wasn't going to let go, but at least he wasn't hurting us.

Yet.

Then, our direction changed. Instead of plummeting down, the creature changed direction and we were now swimming sideways, skirting the tops of tall, dark seaweed and large rocks. Up ahead, I could make out the dark shadowy form of what must be some sort of a tunnel or cave.

In less than a minute, my suspicions were

confirmed. It was a tunnel, all right. We traveled through it, enveloped by a brief darkness. Then, our surroundings lightened, and the creature once again changed direction, this time angling straight up. I could see the surface above, coming closer, closer, closer still . . . .

Then, we broke the surface in a flurry of splashing and cascading water. The creature released me, then vanished beneath the surface.

Griffin bobbed in the water nearby, spluttering and spitting. Wet hair hung in my eyes, and I raised my hand to pull it away. Once again, I was both shocked and amazed at our surroundings.

"This isn't possible," I whispered as I looked around. *"It's just not possible."*

We were in a jungle.

That's right. We had surfaced in a small pond, surrounded by tropical plants of all shapes and sizes. Some of them resembled palm trees; others looked like no other tree I'd ever seen before in my life. Only a dozen feet away was a white, sandy beach. Light came from the sky above, but there was no sun. Instead, all I could see was a canopy of creamy white. It was so very, very strange.

"I can't believe we're seeing this," Griffin

said. "I mean . . . we're inside the Earth somewhere, aren't we? We never went up. That thing pulled us deep down into the water, into the Earth."

I shook my head. "I know," I replied. "It's just not possible."

We were treading water, waving our hands back and forth and kicking our legs to remain afloat. I started swimming toward the shore, arm over arm, until my feet touched the sandy bottom. Then, I stood and waded to the edge of the beach. Despite the lack of sunshine, the air was very warm and felt very thick and humid.

Griffin followed my actions, and soon, the two of us were standing in the sand at the edge of the water, marveling at our bizarre surroundings. We were soaked, and water dripped from my shirt, shorts, hair, and fingertips.

"It's like a world within the world," Griffin said. "But I don't see where it begins or ends."

I suddenly remembered an old book my dad has on his bookshelf at home. It's called *Journey to the Center of the Earth* by Jules Verne. Dad said that it was written in 1864 and that he had read it as a boy and loved it. He said it was about three men who follow volcanic tubes all the way through the Earth, and they discover an entirely different world. It's not true, of course, but Dad said the story was good and that I should read it sometime.

Now, I wish I had, because Griffin and I were definitely deep in the Earth, and we were definitely in another world of some sort. I didn't think we were at the center of the Earth, but that didn't really matter. All that mattered was that we had gone to WonderSplash for a tour and had made a huge mistake.

"Where *are* we?" Griffin said, repeating his question.

"I don't know," I replied. "All I know is that the same thing happened to both of us when we opened that door. Now, here we are."

"How do we get out of here?" he asked.

"That's another good question," I replied. "Being that we don't know where we are, we don't have a lot to go on."

But I had another question, and I figured that Griffin was wondering the same thing. I wondered what that thing was that grabbed us and pulled us into the water and brought us here. I wondered how we were able to travel through the water for several minutes without needing to breathe, without drowning.

And as I glanced down into the crystal waters, I wondered if there were more creatures, lurking in the depths.

Probably, I thought.

So, for a few minutes, Griffin and I did nothing but look around, staring at our strange surroundings, wondering where on Earth—or, rather, where *in* Earth—we were.

"Well," Griffin finally said. "We're not going to get anywhere by just standing here. I say we take a look around."

He was right. Just standing in one spot wasn't going to help us find a way out.

"What if we tried to swim back the way we

came?" I asked. "I mean . . . we didn't have to breathe. We didn't drown. We can probably go back the same way."

Griffin didn't like that idea. "No way," he said, shaking his head. "Do you remember how dark it was? We'll have no way of knowing which way to go. Besides that, we might run into that thing that grabbed us."

He had a good point. Swimming in darkness would be confusing and scary, especially with that freakazoid creature around.

"Okay," I agreed. "But we're going to have to be careful. This place might be pretty big, and we don't need to get lost."

"You forgot one thing," Griffin said with a grin. "We already *are* lost. We have no idea where we are."

"All the same," I said. "We still have to be careful."

Griffin pointed. "Look," he said. "That looks like some sort of trail."

He was right. There was a thin strip of land

where no trees or brush grew. We walked toward it, and I knelt down.

"Look," I said. "Footprints."

Griffin knelt for a closer look.

"Not footprints," he said, shaking his head. "More like animal tracks."

"I've never seen tracks like these before," I said.

Griffin stood and looked around. "I think we're going to see a lot of things we've never seen before," he said.

As much as I was hoping that he was wrong, we were about to find out that he was one-hundred percent correct. In fact, we were about to find out that unseen eyes were upon us, watching us at that very moment.

"Let's not go too far," I said as we set out along the trail.

"I wish we had a ball of string," Griffin replied. "That way, we could tie one end to a tree and roll it out as we walked. We would be able to follow it back to the place we started, if we had to."

"That would work until the string ran out," I said. "Besides: we already know we can't get out by going through the pond. It probably wouldn't make a difference if we make it back there or not."

"Somewhere, there has to be a door or a passageway," Griffin said. "There has to be more than one way out of this place."

While I agreed with Griffin, I had a few more questions of my own.

Why did that strong wind pull us through the door? What was the actual purpose of WonderSplash? Had other people come through that door, besides us?

There were no clear answers to these questions, and I probably wouldn't have any answers until we made it out of—

Where? I wondered again. *Just where are we? What do we call this place?*

And worst of all: nobody knew where we were, except for the guy organizing the tours. He had stepped away. When he came back, would he notice us missing and report it? Was it possible that people were looking for us right now?

No, probably not. The guy organizing the tours probably thought that we left and had no idea that we'd gone through the door and fallen into another world.

We simply had to face the fact that we were on our own, and the only thing we could do was try to find our own way out.

My soaked clothing clung tightly to my body as I followed Griffin. Sand was caked on my wet sneakers.

Suddenly, Griffin stopped, and I almost bumped into him. He snapped his head around, and his eyes darted back and forth.

"What?" I asked. "Did you see something?"

He shook his head. "No," he replied. "But I think I heard something. Did you hear it?"

"Hear what?"

"Just a snapping sound, like a small branch breaking," Griffin said. "Listen."

We stood motionless, listening, but there was nothing to hear. No breeze ruffled the leaves, no birds chirped. Nothing moved. There were no sounds at all.

I looked up at the empty, cream-colored sky and then glanced at a nearby tree. It looked like a maple, except that the leaves were the size of dinner plates.

And I wondered how the plants grew without sunlight. I knew from my school science class that all plants need the sun for energy in a process called photosynthesis, but I didn't understand all that much about how it worked. If there was no sun, how would the plants grow? It was yet another confusing question to which I had no answer.

We watched. Nothing moved.

"Well," Griffin said as he started walking again. "Must've been my imagination."

It wasn't.

There was a sudden, piercing shriek from above. We turned our heads in time to see an enormous, feathered beast dropping out from his hiding place in a tree. As it came down upon us with giant wings spread wide, I was certain that the creature had one thing on his mind: food!

The bird—at least, that's what I called it at first—lunged down at us with sharp talons splayed out, the way a hawk or an eagle would snare a small animal. I was so shocked that for a split second, I couldn't move.

Then, instinct took over. Fear shocked my brain, and adrenaline surged through my bloodstream. I dove to the right, while Griffin dove to the left, just as the beast lashed out with his long, sharp talons. I fell into a clump of bushes and rolled, covering my head with my hands. And by some small miracle, both Griffin and I were spared. The creature missed both of us, and I looked up in time to see the thing rising back up into the sky in a flurry of powerful wings.

"Madison!" Griffin wailed. "Are you all right?"

I didn't take my eyes off the unbelievable flying monstrosity that continued to rise higher into the creamy white sky. By now, Griffin was on his feet, and he rushed over to me, grabbing me by the arm and helping me up.

"Are you all right?" he repeated.

"Yeah," I said, and we both watched the creature as it made a wide circle, then vanished over the treetops.

"What kind of bird was that?" I asked.

"It looked more like a dinosaur than anything," Griffin said.

"You're right!" I replied. "That's why it looked so fierce. It had a face like a velociraptor or some other awful dinosaur."

"We've got to get out of this place," Griffin

said, and I could hear the urgency in his voice. What we were experiencing was simply impossible and unbelievable, but it was real. Somehow, we'd traveled to a place within the Earth, a place of strange trees and bizarre creatures. If I wasn't so terrified, I would be excited and fascinated.

Sand stuck to my wet clothes, and I tried to brush off as much as I could. Thankfully, I didn't have much sand in my hair.

"We need to find something to use as a weapon," Griffin said, looking around. "That thing might come back."

"And there are probably other creatures, too," I said.

We looked around our immediate surroundings, poking in and around the underbrush. The only things we found were several fist-sized rocks.

"Looks like these are all we've got," Griffin said.

"I feel like we've traveled back to the stone age," I said, rolling the rock around in one hand.

"I think you might be right," Griffin said. "We have no way of knowing where we are. Maybe we actually traveled back in time."

"But that's impossible," I said.

"Flying dinosaurs aren't possible either," he replied as he glanced up at the sky. "They died off millions of years ago. But we were just attacked by one."

I gazed warily up at the hazy whiteness that seemed to go on forever, wondering where a light source could be. If there was no sun, how come we weren't immersed in darkness?

It just didn't make sense. *Nothing* made sense, and the confusion was nearly overwhelming. Would we ever make it out alive? Would I ever see my family again? While I tried not to think these thoughts, it was difficult.

So, I tried to focus on our current problem: finding our way out alive. I told myself that if Griffin and I stuck together, we would find a way out. If we relied on each other, we would succeed.

"Let's keep moving," I said. "If we just stay

here, we're going to be sitting ducks."

"I'd feel a lot better if we had more than these rocks to defend ourselves," Griffin said as we began making our way along the trail. We both paid much more attention to our surroundings, turning our heads to the left and to the right, looking up and down, wary that there might be some other creature lying in wait. I held onto my rock tightly, gripping it in my palm, ready to use it on a moment's notice.

Without warning, Griffin turned around, pushed me to the side, and pulled me down into a clump of brush.

"There's something coming this way!" he hissed. *"Climb into the bushes! We have to hide!"*

My heart was racing as we scrambled into a clump of tall, knotted branches with long, thick leaves. We were on our hands and knees, and limbs scratched at the bare skin of my face and arms. In my right hand, I gripped the rock tightly, supporting myself with my knuckles as I crawled along. And I barely noticed my wet clothing, despite the fact that it was a little uncomfortable to move around in.

We stopped, huddled together in a small, tight mass.

"What did you see?" I whispered.

"I don't know," Griffin whispered back. *"I just saw branches and leaves moving, like something was pushing them. Whatever it is, it's coming this way."*

We waited. It felt like my heart was in my throat. I was breathing heavily, and I hoped that my constant wheezing wouldn't be heard by whatever was coming toward us.

Then:

A noise.

A snapping of a branch.

A soft whisper of swishing leaves.

A crunch.

Then:

A movement nearby.

A bending of branches.

A trembling of leaves.

Close.

Closer.

Closer still.

My heart was hammering, but I held my breath. Griffin and I didn't move a muscle. We remained crouched down, each of us holding our rocks, ready to use them if we had to.

The branches and limbs ceased to tremble. Whatever was moving had stopped only a few feet away, but we were unable to see what it was.

Then, we heard another sound.

Sniffing.

Can he smell us? I wondered.

My palms were sweaty, and the rock was warm and damp in my hand.

More sniffing.

Branches bent.

A twig snapped.

The thing was close enough that I thought I could probably reach out and touch it, but I still couldn't see it through the thick, tangled foliage.

But it kept moving away from us, and I was glad. Whatever it was, it hadn't spotted us. Perhaps it smelled us, which was why it had stopped. Soon, the creature had moved on, and we could no longer see the bending of leaves and limbs as it made its way through the dense jungle.

"*Do you think it's safe?*" I whispered.

"*Safe for what?*" Griffin whispered back. "*We're in some sort of world that we don't understand, with creatures that shouldn't exist. We're not going to be safe until we find a way out of here.*"

"Then, let's keep looking," I said, a bit louder as I stood. "The sooner we find our way out, the better."

We cautiously stepped toward the trail, looking all around, wary of anything that might be watching us or coming our way. Nothing moved.

But as we once again started to follow the trail, Griffin's words kept haunting me.

We're not going to be safe until we find a way out of here.

Danger could be anywhere . . . and at that very moment, it was even closer than we had imagined.

We were still carrying our rocks, but Griffin dropped his when he found a long, heavy stick nearly as tall as he was.

"This will be better than a rock," he said, wielding the branch in front of him like a spear. "If something tries to get us, I can use this to try to keep it away. It's not much, but it's better than nothing."

"Have you ever heard of a place like this existing?" I asked. "Anything from a book or a TV documentary?"

"No," Griffin replied, shaking his head as he continued down the trail with his spear at his side. "Have you?"

I shook my head. "No," I answered. Then, I told him about the book my dad had, *Journey to the Center of the Earth* by Jules Verne. He hadn't heard of it.

"Anyway," I said, "it's not real. Mr. Verne made the whole thing up."

"Well, nobody's making all of this up," Griffin said with a sweeping wave of his hand. "You can't tell me this isn't real."

We continued until we came to the top of a small hill where no trees or plants grew. The ground was hard packed, and we saw no signs of any tracks or footprints.

But it gave us our first real look at just how big of a place we were in. We could see plants and trees for as far as our eyes could see. The sky was a curtain of white, similar to what an overcast day would look like. In fact, I wondered if somehow our minds were playing tricks on us, that maybe we hadn't been taken underwater and underground.

No, I told myself. *It happened, all right. It happened because I know that creatures like the weird frog-lizard thing and that flying dinosaur don't exist. Not on the surface of Earth, anyway.*

"I feel like I'm Christopher Columbus discovering a new country," Griffin said. "We're probably seeing what no other human has seen before."

"I feel like—"

My words were cut short as I was suddenly seized beneath my arms and pulled violently up into the air!

"*Help!*" I wailed, powerless to do anything but look down as Griffin became smaller and smaller as I rose higher and higher into the sky. I lost my grip on the rock I'd been carrying, and it fell away, falling to the ground. I looked up, only to realize that I'd been snared by the vicious, dinosaur-bird.

Griffin, unable to do a thing, could only stare up in hopelessness. His spear wouldn't be any use.

I struggled to break free, then stopped, realizing that if the creature let me go, I would fall from the sky. There was no way I would survive if I hit the ground from that height.

So, the only thing I could do was hold on and think horrible thoughts about where I was being taken and what was going to happen.

Was I going to be lunch for the creature? That was the most terrifying thought of all.

Far below, I could see the tiny shape of Griffin as he began running in an attempt to follow us. Every few moments, he would look up to see where we were and adjust his trek. However, I knew he was having difficulty, because he was forced to leave the path and trudge through the dense leaves and branches.

Just above my head, the beast let out a horrible shriek that both surprised and scared me. I turned my head . . . and that's when I saw the wall.

To say that what I was seeing was a mountain wouldn't be accurate. To the left, in the distance, was a gray stone wall hundreds of feet in the air. However, instead of rising to a point like most mountains, the top of the formation was almost completely flat. The strange, white sky seemed like a flat ceiling, and beneath it, there seemed to be no end to the lush green forest that went on for miles in every direction.

But there was something else that stood out: a small black dot in the wall that, even from far away, looked like it was a hole of some sort, a cave-like opening. And as we drew closer and closer to the wall, it became apparent that was where we were headed.

I looked down, but saw no sign of Griffin. We'd left him behind, far below, in the tangle of leafy trees and bushes. I hoped, however, that he could still see us. I hoped he could see where I was being taken.

As we drew closer to the enormous stone wall, I could now make out jagged features, cliffs and ledges and long, dark cracks that forked like lightning. The beast carrying me let out another shriek and stopped flapping his wings. Instead, he spread them wide, and we glided toward the wall, toward the dark, shadowy opening of the cave. As we drew closer, I began to realize how incredibly fast we were traveling. Still, the dinosaur-bird showed no signs of slowing. He simply kept his wings locked in position, outstretched, riding air currents as we headed closer to the wall, faster and faster.

And although I knew he was headed toward the cave, I also realized something else: we were traveling so fast that there was no way he would be able to stop in time. I didn't know what the horrible creature was up to, but I knew he wasn't stopping, and all I could do was close my eyes and prepare myself for the inevitable collision.

The moment I closed my eyes, I was suddenly jerked backward. Opening my eyes, I was surprised to find that the flying monstrosity was using his powerful wings, flapping furiously, to slow down. With me still in his clutches, he expertly landed at the edge of the cave, shifting me into one single claw. For a moment, I thought he was going to lose his grip and drop me, but he was too strong.

Instead, he landed with one claw, folded his wings in, and set me down at the edge of the cave. He towered above me, looking at me curiously.

And I was absolutely terrified. I had no idea why he had brought me to the cave in the wall, nor did I have any idea what he was going to do with me. I'd assumed that I was going to be his lunch, and maybe that was his plan. If that was the case, I wasn't going to let him eat me. The cave was easily a hundred feet in the air. I'd jump to my death before I'd let the ugly thing have me for a late-morning snack.

While he watched me watching him, I had a moment to study his features. Griffin was right: he really *did* resemble a dinosaur. His head was long and narrow, but unlike a bird, he really didn't have a beak. Just a long snout with a mouth filled with rows of teeth. Still, he was shaped like a bird. He had feathers on his body, but none on his head, resembling a vulture. The creature truly *was* hideous, and I knew I was seeing something that no one else on Earth had ever experienced.

A reptilian vulture, I thought. *That's the only way to describe him.* Had I not been so completely terrified, it would have been kind of exciting to discover some weird creature that no one knew about.

The two of us stood near the edge of the cave, sort of sizing up each other. If he meant to harm me, he gave no indication. He appeared to be more curious than anything, looking me up and down from head to toe.

Then, in a single motion, he turned and slipped off the mouth of the cave, spreading his massive wings and taking flight. I watched him as he soared effortlessly, his wings outstretched and motionless, coasting through the air like a glider. He moved gracefully across the sky, becoming smaller and smaller. Just when I thought he was going to vanish completely, he turned. He circled a few times before suddenly plummeting, dropping from the air like a rock.

It was then that I knew what he was after. *Griffin.*

I was certain that the hideous thing must've spotted Griffin, and the flying monster had dropped from the sky to snare him, just like he'd captured me.

And I know this is going to sound weird, but that's what I was hoping for. Above everything else, I didn't want to be alone. Not here, not in some strange world beneath the surface of the planet. I'd feel much better if Griffin were with me. We could lean on each other for support. Like the saying goes: two heads are better than one.

Inching back from the mouth of the cave, I searched the sky, looking for some sign of the flying reptile. Hoping to see him growing larger as he approached, hoping to see Griffin in his clutches.

But I didn't.

All I could see for miles and miles was the creamy white sky above and the ocean of leafy green vegetation below.

The minutes ticked past. I saw no sign of the strange, flying beast and no sign of Griffin. No sign of any life at all.

I was all alone, on my own, in a world I knew nothing about. A world filled with strange monsters and beasts. A world within a world, a dangerous place that shouldn't exist.

Things had just gone from bad . . . to worse.

"Stay calm," I quietly told myself. *"Just stay calm, and everything is going to be all right."*

I'm not sure if I even believed myself, but just thinking those words did make me feel a little better.

So, instead of panicking and thinking dark thoughts, I sat down to think. I'd made several glances into the dark cave behind me, and I wondered if I should explore a bit. The tunnel might lead to a way out.

But after thinking about it more, I decided

not to. It was too dark, and once I was a few dozen feet from the mouth of the cave, I wouldn't be able to see anything.

I sat with my legs crossed, gazing off into the distance, wondering what to do. I was way, way too high to jump, and I certainly couldn't climb up or down the face of the wall.

And no one was going to come to my rescue, that was for sure.

"Stay calm," I repeated to myself. *"Just stay calm, and everything is going to be all right."*

My clothes were beginning to dry, so my shirt and jeans didn't feel so clammy and uncomfortable. And most of the sand had fallen off, too.

All the while, my eyes kept scanning the creamy sky and the tangle of jungle below, searching for movement, hoping to see some sign of Griffin. And hoping that I didn't see any signs of anything else. We'd already encountered three creatures. One bizarre frog-lizard creature, and one that resembled a cross between a dinosaur and a bird. And the other creature we'd encountered? We had no idea what he looked like, as we'd been hiding in the bushes.

As the minutes passed, my situation grew more hopeless. I began to wonder if perhaps I *should* venture deeper into the cave. Maybe the cave would lead somewhere.

Then again, I was afraid of what I might find. Was it the home of the flying beast that had kidnapped and brought me here? Was he going to return? Maybe there were more just like him, deeper in the cave. I had no way of knowing, unless I found out for myself.

I peered cautiously into the darkness, trying to make out any shapes or forms in the murky gloom. I saw nothing.

I took a step forward, but stopped when I heard something.

No, not something. Some*one*.

A voice.

A voice!

It was distant, but it was definitely a human

voice . . . and it was definitely Griffin!

I turned around and looked down. My jaw dropped. I stared in disbelief.

Griffin, without any means of support, was rising from the ground and floating upward, toward me!

I couldn't believe it. I *refused* to believe it. My eyes simply had to be playing tricks on me.

While I watched, Griffin rose higher and higher into the air, drifting up as gracefully as a helium balloon! As he drew nearer, I could see that he was making sweeping motions with his arms and kicking his legs, as if he was swimming.

How is he doing that? I wondered in amazement. *How is he defying gravity and rising into the air like he's a feather, carried by a gust of wind?*

It wasn't possible, but I knew what I was seeing. My mind wasn't playing tricks on me.

He continued to rise, up, up, into the air, drifting closer and closer to me. He was smiling as he made his way toward the cave, propelling himself along by using easy swimming motions with his hands, arms, and legs.

"How are you doing that?" I shouted to him.

"Isn't this cool?!?!" he shouted back.

"But . . . but . . . how . . . ," I stammered, still completely baffled at the sight of my new friend rising effortlessly in the air.

When he was only a few yards away, I took a step back from the ledge, and he gently came to rest in the very spot where I had been standing.

"How . . . how did you . . . ," I stammered again. I was so confused and baffled that I couldn't even get a complete sentence out.

Griffin raised one hand to his mouth and pulled out a wad of what appeared to be gum. It was pink and fleshy and wet.

"Easy," he said. "With this." He held out the

chewed pink and red blob for me to see.

"Gum?" I asked.

Griffin shrugged. "I guess so. I was getting hungry, and I found a tree that had these growing on it."

With his free hand, he dug into a front pocket and produced a large berry. It was red and about the size of a small crab apple.

"I took a bite, and it tasted good," Griffin said. "Sweet and tangy, almost like candy. So, I popped the whole thing into my mouth. But instead of breaking down, it became rubbery and chewy. That's when I realized I was feeling lighter and lighter. I moved my arms a little and rose up off the ground! I was so freaked out that I spit out the gum. When I did, I floated back to the ground."

"So, while you chew the gum, you can actually fly?" I asked.

Griffin nodded. "Yep," he said. "And when you take it out, the effect wears off. Try it."

He handed me the berry, and I rolled it over in my hand. I sniffed it, but it had no smell whatsoever.

"It's impossible," I said.

"Hey," Griffin said. "Everything that's happened to us is impossible. Being kidnapped by a weird creature, not drowning in the water, taken to a world within the Earth, you being caught and taken away by some sort of flying dinosaur. Everything we've experienced so far shouldn't be happening. So, gum that lets you fly doesn't seem all that farfetched."

I stared at the red berry in my hand.

"Go ahead, try it," Griffin urged. He popped his wad of gum back into his mouth and began to chew. Then, with a gentle flap of his arms, he rose a few inches in the air. To remain there, hovering like he was, all he needed to do was sweep his arms back and forth, forward and backward, as if he was treading water.

"It's fun!" he said with a wide smile. "Try it!"

Slowly, I put the entire fruit into my mouth and rolled it around. Then, cautiously, I bit down and began to chew. I was surprised by its sharp sweetness. It was tangy and juicy, just like Griffin said. But instead of breaking down into smaller pieces, the morsel became rubbery and chewy.

And a strange feeling came over me. I began to feel lighter, weightless.

"Flap your arms just a little," Griffin said.

Although it seemed silly, I did as he asked and was amazed to find that my feet left the ground! It really felt as if I was swimming in the air!

"Watch this," Griffin said, and with a slow sweep of his arms, he spun himself upside down!

"It's like being in space," I said as I looked down at my feet. They were several inches from the flat, rocky ground. "It's like there isn't any gravity."

"Now, take the gum out of your mouth," he instructed. I did, holding the chewed wad in my hand. The moment it left my mouth, I began to feel heavier, and I floated back to solid ground.

"This is crazy!" I said with a laugh, then popped the gum back into my mouth and began to chew. The moment I did, I waved my arms and rose into the air again.

"I know!" Griffin replied. "I haven't had much time to experiment, but it sure is cool. Are you afraid of heights?"

"Not really," I replied. "But if you're going to ask me to step off of this ledge and into thin air, I don't think I can do it."

"Sure you can!" Griffin said. With another easy wave of his arms, he righted himself, and then made swimming motions. He floated off and over the ledge and into empty space, suspended in the air a hundred feet above the ground.

"Come on," he said. "It's the only way to get down from up here."

Floating a few inches above the solid footing of the ledge, I looked down into the lush, green forest far below. My mind seemed to be arguing with itself. One side said that if I were to move off the safety of the ledge, I would plummet to my death.

And yet, here I was, floating in mid-air.

"You can do it," Griffin urged.

Slowly, I reached out with both arms, as if I was swimming. I'm not the least bit afraid to admit that it was a terrifying experience, for I had suddenly left the safety of the ledge and drifted out into the air, weightless, with the green jungle now hundreds of feet below.

"You're doing it!" Griffin said. "That's it! Come out a little more!"

I cupped my palms as if scooping water, except I was scooping air. Pulling them back pushed me forward, and I nearly bumped into Griffin.

"Follow me," he said, and he turned upside down and began to 'swim' downward. I followed his movements, and soon, I was slowly pulling myself downward in a gentle dive, straight down. I was still a bit horrified at being so high off the ground—but it was nothing compared to the horror I was about to feel . . . .

We had no way of knowing that trouble was brewing, and fast. Griffin and I were so totally focused on our slow descent, so awed and amazed at being weightless, that we failed to look around. We were totally focused on the ground below as we gently floated lower and lower.

So, when we heard a piercing shriek nearby, both of us were shocked. We turned to see the horrible dinosaur-bird dropping out of the sky with incredible speed. His wings were folded in, and he was like a live torpedo, aiming for the two of us.

I screamed and began swimming sideways in the air, turning my body to face the terrifying attacker. Moving was awkward. I had no idea how much I relied on gravity every waking second of the day. I truly felt as if I was in a pool or a lake, without anything to grasp or hold.

Still, I managed to face our attacker. Griffin had dove straight down, putting distance between us. The only question now was who the beast was going to go after . . . me or Griffin?

I cupped my hands and spread my arms wide, then pushed forward. The motion propelled me backward, and I did it again and again until my back was against the wall.

The terrifying dinosaur-bird was still coming and had set his sights on me.

Again.

But with my back against the rock wall, I now had a plan. If I couldn't use gravity, perhaps I could use my muscle to make a move that would surprise the creature, allowing me to escape. Or at the very least, give me a fighting chance of escaping.

I glanced up at the approaching dinosaur-bird, estimating that I would have about ten seconds before he would be upon me. Looking to my left and then to my right, I found a small ledge. With a quick sweep of my right hand, I was inverted, upside down, against the wall. I put both feet against the bottom of the ledge and tucked myself into an upside down ball.

Five seconds.

Four.

Three.

Two . . .

Just as the huge beast spread his wings to slow himself, as he positioned his talons out front to snatch me, I pushed from the bottom of the ledge with every ounce of strength I had. The effort sent me sailing downward, head first. I didn't bother to turn my head to see where the awful flying monster was or what happened to him, but I knew from his angry shriek that he wasn't happy that I'd escaped.

And I was amazed at how fast I was moving! My push away from the ledge really sent me sailing downward fast, as if I was actually falling. At the speed I was going, I would overtake Griffin in a matter of seconds.

But that's where things became a problem. I was headed right for him at a tremendous speed. I spread my arms out to slow myself down, flapping them like a bird, but it had little effect. I was slowing down, but not fast enough.

"Griffin!" I shouted. *"Watch out! I'm going to hit you!"*

Griffin was still diving straight down, and he bent his head and looked up at me . . . at the very same moment that my body slammed into him. The impact slowed my movement a lot; I was hovering in the air, nearly motionless. Griffin had been knocked sideways by the impact, and the hit had stopped his downward movement.

We were both dazed, but only for a moment. Then, Griffin's eyes grew wide.

"My gum!" he shouted. "My gum was

knocked out of my mouth when you hit me!"

At first, I didn't understand what he meant.

But then, he began to sink, slowly at first, and then faster.

"My gum!" he shrieked. *"I can't float without my gum!"*

Suddenly, Griffin was in a free fall, plummeting from the sky, his legs and arms flailing like an overturned beetle, plunging down, down, racing toward what would certainly be instant death.

And it was all my fault.

23

I felt horrible, but there was absolutely nothing I could do. I had hit Griffin, and the force of the strike had caused his gum to be knocked from his mouth. Without the gum, he was no longer able to float in the air, and now he was tumbling helplessly to the ground below.

The only good thing about the situation was that the awful dinosaur-bird had fled. He didn't mount another attack, and when I snapped my head around to see where he was, I saw him flying off into the distance.

But beneath me, Griffin was falling faster and faster. Using one arm, I inverted myself, trying to pull myself down. I moved painfully slow, and I knew there was no way I would be able to reach him in time. I would never be able to catch up to him.

But what if—

Without thinking anything more about it, I reached up and plucked the gum from my mouth, holding it carefully between my thumb and forefinger. Immediately, I began to sink. Slowly at first, but in seconds, I, too, was in a dead free fall, rocketing down toward the ground.

Still, I knew I wasn't going to be able to catch up to Griffin. He had gotten too much of a head start, and even though I was now racing toward the ground, he was going to beat me to it. Unfortunately, he had no way of stopping himself. As for me, all I had to do was put the gum back into my mouth and start chewing, and I would slow down and become buoyant again.

I continued to fall faster and faster. The rush

of air in my face caused my eyes to water, and my vision blurred. I could no longer see Griffin, and I knew that he would be slamming into the ground at any second. I also knew that there was no way he was going to survive an impact like that. I'd known him less than twenty-four hours . . . and now he was gone forever. He was gone, and I was once again alone in a strange, bizarre world.

I popped the wad of gum back into my mouth and began to chew. The effect was immediate, and I suddenly began to slow. The more I chewed, the slower I went.

I wiped my eyes on the sleeve of my shirt and looked down.

Impossible!

I couldn't believe it, but Griffin was below me. Not only was he below me, but he appeared to be stationary, just sort of hanging in the air like a cloud. He was looking up at me as I slowly descended.

"I thought you were gone forever!" I shouted to him. "I thought you were going to slam into the ground at a million miles an hour!"

"I had another one of those berries in my pocket," Griffin explained. By now, I had reached his altitude, and the two of us used our arms to remain balanced in the air, facing each other.

"I had a hard time reaching it," Griffin continued, "because I was twisting and turning so much. I was finally able to grab it and put it in my mouth."

"I'm so glad you're alive," I said.

"Me, too," Griffin said with a cheeky grin. "Getting killed would have really messed up my day."

I laughed. "In case you haven't noticed, our day is already messed up. It's messed up a whole lot."

"Things could be worse," Griffin said, and I immediately wished he wouldn't have said those words. He was right, for sure. Things could get much worse . . . and they were about to.

Inverting ourselves like divers, we began swinging our arms in swimming motions to slowly pull us toward the ground. Soon, we were both standing next to one another. Both of us spit out our gum, and I quickly felt the gravitational pull of the Earth, keeping my feet firmly planted on the ground. While I thought that the gum was pretty cool, I felt much better on solid land. Still, those mysterious berries might come in handy again.

"Do you have any more of those things?" I asked.

"You mean the berries?" replied Griffin.

"Yeah."

He shook his head. "No," he answered. "But I saw a few other trees with the same kind of fruit. Why?"

"We should probably have some, just in case we need them again."

Griffin looked around. We'd 'landed' in a small clearing of tall grass. Around us, trees of various kinds grew. Some were tall and thin, spiraling upward like pines; others were short and squatty.

"That's probably a good idea," Griffin said. "It shouldn't be too hard to find more."

"What we need is a magical berry that will take us back to the waterpark," I said.

"Yeah," Griffin agreed. "But I don't think that's going to happen."

I followed him through the grass to a tree.

"They should be easy to find," he said, "because the berries are red and stand out against the green leaves."

It didn't take us long to find one of the trees with the shiny red fruit. We each plucked a couple of berries and stuffed them into our pockets.

"Now what?" I asked, looking around.

"We've got to keep hunting for a way out of here," Griffin replied.

"What if we chewed some gum and went to the top of the rock wall?" I asked. "We'll be so high up, we might see something. We might find our way out."

Griffin's eyes lit up. "That's a great idea!" he said, and he looked up, scanning the sky. "We'll have to keep a watch out for that ugly flying thing, though."

"And we should have something to defend ourselves, in case he comes back," I said.

We searched and searched, but the only things we found were a few small rocks and a couple of branches . . . hardly anything that would be useful if that flying dinosaur thing attacked again.

"I guess we'll just have to take our chances,"

Griffin said as he dropped a small rock he'd picked up. "There's nothing here that's going to be of any use to us."

I popped one of my berries into my mouth and began chewing. Instantly, I felt lighter, and with an easy wave of my arms, I was rising into the air. Griffin floated next to me.

"These things would be worth a fortune!" he said. "When we get home and show people what we've discovered, we're going to be rich!"

"And famous," I said.

"Yeah," Griffin echoed. "Rich and famous. That's going to be awesome!"

I smiled, but I wasn't so sure Griffin was right. Oh, I wouldn't mind being rich and all that, but being famous? I don't think I would like that. Famous people are always being hounded by photographers and journalists. When you're famous, you don't really get a lot of privacy. I didn't think I would like that.

Regardless, that wasn't something to worry about at the time. We needed to focus on getting out of this place and back to the waterpark. And our best chance was to fly to the top of the rock wall where, no doubt, we'd be able to see for miles. Hopefully, we might discover a way out of this strange world.

With amazing ease, we continued to rise into the air. It was the most incredible sight to see Griffin rising into the air, weightless, pulling himself higher and higher with gentle strokes of his arms. It was still a little unnerving to see the ground dropping away from me, but I felt so light that my concerns about falling vanished. I knew that as long as I had the gum in my mouth, I was safe. And both Griffin and I had a spare berry in our pockets, just in case.

And I was feeling pretty good. So far, we'd survived. We were alive, and I was more and more confident that we would find our way out.

But we were also about to find that a new nightmare awaited us at the top of the rock wall.

While we continued our climb into the sky, Griffin and I were careful to turn our heads and be on alert for any potential threat, especially that crazed dinosaur-bird. It made me more than a little nervous, being that we had no way to defend ourselves and nowhere to go. And it would be impossible, I was sure, to fly faster than him.

By now, our clothing was mostly dry, and it was much more comfortable to move around. My skin didn't feel as if it were constantly rubbing up against wet sandpaper.

Higher and higher we rose toward the white sky, and I again wondered where the light source was coming from. Since there was no sun, there shouldn't be any light at all. After all: when the sun sets, it gets dark. It's as simple as that.

But I had to remind myself that we were in a totally different world. Everything was different, from the plants and animals, to the water and the sky. It was as if Griffin and I had traveled to another planet.

Slowly, we approached the top of the massive rock wall. Below us, everything looked small. Far off, I could see what appeared to be a small lake. I gave one more sweep with both arms, and it was enough to gently propel me up to the top of the rock wall, where I was getting my first glimpse of what it looked like. Griffin, too, had reached the top, and we grasped the ledge and easily pulled ourselves onto it. Then, when we were safely on its flat surface, I pulled the wad of gum from my mouth. Griffin did the same, and gravity once again held us firmly on the rock plane.

"Wow," Griffin said and gave out a low whistle. "I can't believe how far we can see."

In every direction, we could see the horizon, a gauzy line where the green foliage met the creamy sky.

As far as the rock wall was concerned, the top of it was flat. Not far away, there were two very large holes that were about as big around as the cave in the side of the wall. One side of the wall—the side we'd traveled up—was steep and vertical. However, the other side was more mountainous, sloping down over a long grade.

"Hold everything," Griffin said as he pointed off into the distance. "What's that?"

I looked where he was pointing and saw a dot in the sky, far away. It appeared to be headed in our direction.

"I'll bet it's that ugly flying dinosaur," I said.

"We've got to hide!" Griffin said. His head snapped around. "Over there! Those big holes!"

We raced to the nearest hole in the rock. It

was large, about as big around as a small car, and it was deep. The only thing we could see when we looked down was endless darkness, like a deep, black well.

"Perfect," Griffin said, popping his wad of gum back into his mouth. "Let's just float down a little bit and wait for that thing to fly over. If he's looking for us, he won't see us down there."

That seemed like a good idea. We could hide in the dark hole, suspended in the air, while the dinosaur-bird passed by.

Unfortunately, it never even occurred to us that there might be something inside the hole.

Something that was much, much worse than the ugly flying dinosaur.

I put my wad of gum in my mouth and began to chew, instantly feeling the Earth's gravitational pull begin to fade away. I stepped over the hole with one cautious foot, then the other, and I remained there for a moment, floating, still not quite used to the feeling of weightlessness.

Then, I spread my arms out from my side, held my hands palms up, and raised them quickly. The movement sent my body slowly sinking downward, down into the darkness of the hole. Griffin followed my actions, and in only a few seconds we were nearly twenty feet down.

"Think this is far enough?" I asked as I stopped moving my arms in an upward motion and began to slowly wave them in front of me to keep my body floating in the same place.

"Probably," Griffin replied, coming to a stop a few feet from me. "Let's just wait here for a while."

We remained in that position for about ten minutes, our heads cocked back and our eyes up, searching for the flying beast. We saw no sign of him.

"I'll go take a look," Griffin said. "Hang tight."

Which was kind of an odd thing to say, because I wasn't 'hanging tight' to anything. I was just floating in the darkness, slowly moving my arms back and forth in front of me in a treading water motion.

With gentle arm strokes, Griffin rose slowly. When he neared the opening, he placed his hands on the rock wall to slow his movements. Using the wall, he slowly crawled to the top, cautiously peering up and all around. Then, he looked down at me.

"I don't see anything," he said. "I think we're safe to—"

He stopped speaking, and I thought his eyes were going to bulge out of his head.

"What?" I asked him. "What's the matter!"

"Beneath you!" Griffin shrieked. "It's right beneath you!"

I looked down into the shadowy darkness, face to face with what could only be a giant snake. His eyes were the size of volleyballs, and his head nearly filled the entire tunnel.

Then, he opened his mouth . . . .

27

The snake lunged for me, and the only thing that saved me was his snout. I had been able to turn just in time, and his strike was off a few inches. Instead of swallowing me whole, his nose hit my feet. Without any gravitational pull, the sudden impact sent me flying up past Griffin and into the sky like a kicked football.

And Griffin wasn't going to waste any time fleeing. He pulled himself from the hole, braced his feet on the solid surface, crouched, and leapt. He, like me, shot up into the air.

And he was just in time, too. The snake continued his assault, and if Griffin had waited just another moment, the snake would have devoured him.

And what a monstrous reptile he was! He looked like many of the boa constrictors I'd seen on television and in pictures, except he was easily twenty times the size of the biggest one I'd ever seen! He had a gargantuan, bulb-shaped head and was light brown with darker brown and black splotches.

He exploded from the hole like a rocket, stretching fifty feet in the air before he reared his head back. His body, much of it still concealed in the hole, writhed and twisted. He opened his mouth, displaying a long, forked tongue.

And his eyes! I'd never seen such hatred in any creature. Even the nasty dinosaur-bird didn't look as ferocious as the beefy reptile threatening us.

Griffin and I rose higher and higher, safely out of harm's way. I shuddered when I remembered that I'd been stranded near the cave in the side of the wall, and now I realized that, had I entered through the tunnel to find another way out, I probably would have encountered this monstrosity of a creature . . . and the end result wouldn't have been good.

"That thing nearly gave me a heart attack!" Griffin shouted. We were now quite high above the snake, which was already retreating into his hole.

"He almost swallowed me in one gulp!" I replied. "I had to kick myself away from him when he hit me with his nose!"

"We really have to find a way out of here," Griffin said. "Everywhere we go, we're being attacked by weird creatures. We're both lucky to still be alive."

I looked up. "You know," I said, "we've never explored the sky. If we're inside the Earth, we must be in some sort of gigantic cave. There must be a ceiling of some sort."

Griffin looked up. "It's worth a shot," he said. Then, he looked down. "I hope I don't lose my gum now," he said.

"Me, too," I said, and I quickly felt my right front pocket to make sure that I still had my spare fruit. I did.

Griffin and I continued to rise, and everything below became very small. I must say that I was a bit nervous about being so far up in the sky, but the sensation of being weightless was very powerful. I felt lighter than a feather, so I really didn't have a fear of falling. I knew from experience, however, that everything would change if I didn't have my gum in my mouth.

What a bizarre world this is, I thought again.

"Wait a minute," Griffin said. He stopped moving his arms, and I did, too.

"What?" I asked.

"I don't think we're going any higher," he said. "I've been looking down, and it doesn't seem like we're moving."

I looked up. "The sky looks the same as always. It hasn't changed, and it doesn't appear to be solid."

"If we're going to find a way out," Griffin said, "I don't think it's going to be up here. Let's head back down."

With a sweep of my arm, I was upside down, pulling myself downward. The sensation was exactly like swimming, and I must say the experience was a lot of fun.

As we descended, I looked for the giant wall where we'd been attacked by the huge snake. I didn't want to get anywhere near that place again!

But I was also careful to take in everything else. I spotted what appeared to be several lakes. Mostly, though, the only thing I could see was an endless, green jungle.

Then, I spotted something else.

At first, I thought it was a large boulder near a lake. But there was something about it that attracted my attention. It was too smooth, too uniform. Too man-made looking. It was a deep, blue-green color and very large.

"What's that?" I said, pointing to the object.

"I don't know," Griffin replied.

As we continued to sink down, closer and closer to the ground, it became obvious that what we were looking at was most certainly constructed by humans. It was the mouth of a large cave that went into the Earth. A trickle of water flowed from the bottom, emptying into the lake.

"Wait a minute!" I exclaimed. "That color! That texture! That's the same color as the big slide in the waterpark!"

"It must be connected somehow!" Griffin said. "That's our way out of here!"

Which, of course, it was. But just because we'd found something connected to the waterpark didn't necessarily mean that we were out of danger.

And we were about to learn that the hard way.

We drifted down to the mouth of the wide opening, which appeared to be made from the same material used to make the slides and rides at WonderSplash. It was probably ten feet in diameter, so it was plenty big enough for Griffin and me to walk inside. And the water draining from the oversized pipe was only a trickle, not enough to even come over our sneakers.

My gum was getting harder in my mouth and had long ago lost its taste. I spit it out. If I needed to fly again, I had more in my pocket.

Griffin spit out his, too, and our feet gently touched down at the mouth of the large pipe.

"This has to be the way out!" he said. "I'm sure this giant pipe must connect to the waterpark. We might have to follow it back in the dark."

"We'll probably be safer in there than out here," I said.

"I think you're right," Griffin said.

We climbed up into the oversized pipe. I took one last look at the strange world we'd experienced, and I hoped that when we got out, we'd have some answers. I wanted to know why this weird world beneath the Earth's surface existed. How long had it been hidden? How many more strange and incredible creatures did it contain? Was there anyone who knew about the place besides us?

There must be, I thought. *We were pulled through that door. There must be others who know about this strange place.*

"I wonder how far we'll have to walk," Griffin said, and his voice sounded hollow in the confines of the large plastic pipe.

"I can't imagine it'll be too far," I said. "If this pipe is connected to WonderSplash, it's probably some sort of drain."

We started walking.

"I just can't figure any of this out," I said. "I've been thinking and thinking, but nothing I come up with makes sense."

"Same here," Griffin agreed. "I have a billion questions and no answers."

The farther we continued into the drain, the darker it became. Finally, there was no light at all. I kept bumping into Griffin, and he kept bumping into me, until I finally found his hand in the darkness and held onto it.

"Gee," Griffin quipped, and I could hear his smile through the tone of his voice. "I didn't think you liked me so much."

I laughed. "Oh, I like you just fine," I said. "But I'm tired of bumping into you."

From there on, walking wasn't so bad. We were able to stay in the middle of the pipe, because if we journeyed too far to the left or right, we could feel the curving incline.

We walked for about ten minutes in total darkness. And then—

"Is that a light up ahead?" Griffin said.

It was! Ahead of us, I could see a faint, gray gloom. We began to walk faster. The light got brighter and brighter. The pipe made a sharp turn, and suddenly, we had reached our journey's end. We'd reached the end of the pipe, but it wasn't open like the other end. This end had an iron grate crisscrossing the entire end, and the spaces between weren't big enough for us to squeeze through. A small stream of water trickled through the opening and swirled past our shoes.

On the other side of the grate was what appeared to be an empty pool, and on the other side of that was yet another pipe with iron bars.

"Dead end," Griffin said. "We're stuck."

Then: hope. A man appeared at the edge of the empty pool. He was standing next to a large lever.

"Hey!" I shouted. "Hey! Help! Help us!" I waved my arms and yelled several more times.

But the man didn't hear me. Instead, he grabbed the lever and pulled it back.

"Hey!" I shouted, and Griffin joined in. "Help! We're over here!"

The pipe began to tremble faintly, and we stopped shouting.

"What's going on?" I asked.

And in the next moment, I got my answer. At the other end of the empty pool, a huge wall of water began pouring from the other pipe and through the iron bars. It quickly rushed into the pool, a massive wall of churning liquid and foam . . . which meant that it was heading for us.

Griffin's words echoed in my head.

Dead end.

He was right. We'd reached a—

Dead end.

We turned and ran. Oh, I knew that it was pointless, that there would be no way of outrunning the mad rush of water, but we weren't going to just stand there and be swept away.

The problem was, when we retreated, the light faded. Within seconds, we were in total darkness. It became impossible to run fast, as we couldn't see where we were going.

But the huge wall of water that should have overtaken us never came. I tripped over Griffin's leg and nearly fell, then I stopped running. I could hear his footsteps as he continued to flee.

"Griffin, wait!" I shouted.

His footsteps stopped.

"Come on!" I heard him shout in the darkness.

"I don't hear any water," I said.

"That's impossible," Griffin replied. His voice was closer now, as he was walking back toward me in the dark pipe.

"Listen," I said.

"I don't hear anything," said Griffin.

"That's my point," I insisted. "The water should have reached us by now."

We changed direction and walked cautiously back through the darkness until we saw the glow up ahead. The iron bars of the grate came back into our vision, but on the other side of it, water was up over our heads. It was like looking into a giant aquarium.

"Wait a minute," I said as I approached the steel bars. "Look closer. There's a pane of glass a few feet on the other side of this grate. We didn't see it before, because it was completely see-through and invisible. The thick glass is holding the water back."

"It's almost like looking into an aquarium," Griffin said.

"Or a pool of some sort," I said. "It must be part of—"

There was a sudden scraping sound above, and light flooded down as a square hole opened in the pipe above us. Griffin and I jumped, and we each took a step back, looking up at the scariest looking man I had ever seen in my life.

When I saw the man glaring down at us, one word came to mind:

Crazy.

His hair was black and messy and looked like a bird's nest. He wore thick, round spectacles that gave him a bug-like appearance. He hadn't shaved in a couple of days, and there was a film of thick gristle coating his cheeks and chin, with a thin strip forming a mustache between his upper lip and nose.

And he had a scowl that caused a shiver to

run down my spine. I almost turned and ran, but I realized that, however crazy he might be, he was perhaps the only person who could help us out of this strange, underground world.

"I thought I heard voices! What are you two children doing down there?!?!" he demanded.

Griffin and I said nothing. I think we were too stunned to speak.

"Well?" the man continued. "Cat got your tongue? I asked you a question! What are you two doing down there? How did you—"

"We . . . we don't know," I stammered.

The man looked puzzled. "What on earth do you mean?" he asked. "Why don't you know?"

"Just like Madison said," Griffin replied, coming to my defense. "We *don't know* what we're doing here. We accidentally got sucked through a door. That's how this whole thing got started."

"That's right," I replied. "All we want to do is get out of here."

"Stay right there," the man ordered. "Don't move."

The man vanished, and I looked at Griffin. "Who do you think he is?" I asked.

Griffin shook his head. "I have no idea," he replied, "but he looks like he's crazy."

"You can say that again," I said. "I don't think he's combed his hair in years."

We heard some banging around up above. Soon, the man returned carrying a ladder. He slipped it through the open rectangle. Griffin reached for it and planted the two legs firmly at our feet, then checked to make sure it was solid.

Finally! I thought. *We're finally getting out of here!*

Griffin motioned toward me. "Go ahead," he said, and I didn't waste any time. I grasped a rung with both hands, took a step up, and quickly hustled up the ladder. When I was near the top of the pipe, the man reached down and helped pull me out. Griffin was right behind me, and the man helped him, too.

We were in a large room containing a deep, rectangular pool. The ceiling was high, inlaid with a dozen long, tubular florescent lights.

The man looked at me, then Griffin, then back to me. "Who wants to tell me how you wound up down there?"

Griffin and I both started talking at once, and the man raised his hands to silence us. Then, he pointed at me. "You first."

I explained how Griffin was looking for a restroom, and a hurricane-force wind sucked him through a doorway. When I went to help him, the same thing happened to me. Griffin and I then took turns telling the man everything we'd experienced. He showed no emotion, no surprise or shock. Rather, he appeared intensely interested.

"You are both very lucky," the man said. "The doorway you were pulled through was not intended for people to go through. You see, beneath the waterpark, the air pressure is much different, but it changes often. The door allows us to control the air pressure if it gets too high or low."

I didn't know exactly what he was talking

about, but I kept listening.

"That door should have been locked. In fact, it wasn't built for humans to open it manually. A computer automatically senses the air pressure beneath and will open the door on its own, at night, when there is no one else around."

"But why build a waterpark?"Griffin asked.

"The waterpark was built to keep people from discovering the new world. At least, not until the world is ready."

Griffin and I looked at each other.

"But . . . but just what *is* that place?" I stammered.

"We still don't know ourselves," the strange-looking man said. "We don't know enough about it. All we know is that it goes against anything we've learned about the history of the Earth, about geology, biology, anthropology . . . everything. The passageway to this hidden world was discovered only two years ago. We knew that if word got out, thousands upon thousands of people would descend upon the area. We know from history that such a massive onslaught of well-meaning, curious people could quite possibly destroy the ecosystem of the new world."

"Who's 'we?'" Griffin asked.

"SOCRATES," the man replied.

"SOCRATES?" I echoed.

The man nodded. "Yes," he said. "It stands for *Society of Concerned Researchers Assigned to Environmental Sciences.* We're a top-secret group of some of the world's smartest scientists. When we received word that this new, underground world was discovered, we knew that we must somehow protect it. As far as we know, the only entrance is through a strange waterway that bores deep into the Earth, although the water is unlike any other water on Earth. The water molecules contain high amounts of oxygen, allowing creatures—and humans—to absorb air and breathe through their skin."

"That's why we didn't drown!" I said. "We got dragged into the water by an ugly, giant toad, and I thought we were going to drown. But we didn't."

"That 'toad,' as you called him, isn't a toad at all. As far as we can tell, he's closely related to the Apachesaurus, an amphibian thought to exist in the late-Triassic era."

"They sure are scary looking," I said.

"Yes, indeed they are," the man said. "But what little research we've done on them tells us that they are quite harmless. In fact, they are rather playful pranksters."

"You mean," Griffin said, "when that thing grabbed us and pulled us into the water, he was only *playing?*"

The man nodded. "Most likely," he said. "Oh, I admit they do look quite dreadful. But from what we can gather, they're not dangerous at all. There are many, many species in this new inner world within the Earth, most of which SOCRATES have yet to study. Which is why we built the waterpark. We needed a 'disguise' to protect this discovery from the outside world."

"Sort of like hiding it in plain sight," I said.

The man's wide eyes lit up. "Exactly!" he said. "No one—absolutely no one—can know of this place."

"Nobody?" Griffin asked.

The man looked glum as he shook his head. He looked at Griffin, then at me, and spoke. What he said sent a wave of terror washing through my body, and I realized that our nightmare wasn't over; in fact, it was just beginning.

"Nobody," the man said. "Which is why we cannot allow either one of you to leave this place. *Ever.*"

I blinked.

Did he just say what I thought he said? I thought. *Did he just say that we can never leave?*

"What do you mean?" Griffin asked.

"You're children," the man said. "If we allow you to leave, there's too much of a risk of you telling someone. No one must know, and we've all been sworn to secrecy. This new waterpark will bring thousands and thousands of people, and not a single one of them will know that they are frolicking on top of one of the most important discoveries in the history of mankind. If one—just one person—were to find out about this place, it would jeopardize everything we've worked for. We need to study what we've found, find out more about it, make plans to protect this new world. Then, and only then, can we make an announcement to the rest of humanity."

"But . . . but you can't kidnap us!" I stated, nearly shouting. "That's illegal! People will be looking for us, and you'll get into a lot of trouble."

Now it was the man's turn to blink. He stroked his chin and spoke.

"Yes, yes," he said. "I guess I hadn't thought about that. We definitely can't break the law, but we must make sure that word of our discovery doesn't get out."

"We won't tell anyone," Griffin said. He shook his head. "And besides: who would believe us?"

"But how can I be sure?" the man said. "What if it just 'slips out?' Or worse: what if you decide to share your secret with a trusted friend, but that person spills the beans? No, no, we can't have that. Our discovery is far too important."

"Wait a minute!" I said. "I have an idea!"

Griffin and the man looked at me.

"Why don't we just tell everyone?" I asked.

The man's jaw dropped, and Griffin flinched.

"Tell everyone?!?!" the man said. "That's preposterous!"

"Hang on, hang on," I said. "What if I write a bunch of notes about everything we've discovered, and it's published in a book?"

The man looked even more incredulous. "I just finished telling you that no one must know!" he exclaimed. "You've gone barking mad!"

"No, I haven't," I said. "Think about it: you've built a waterpark right on top of the entrance to this new world you've discovered. You're hiding it in plain sight. No one will ever suspect there's a strange, undiscovered world right beneath their feet."

"But we can't publish what we've found in a book!" the man insisted.

"Of course we can!" I said. "All we need to do is get that one guy who writes those scary books for kids—the guy who wears those funny, googly glasses—to write the story. It would make a great book, and no one—nobody—would ever suspect it's a true story!"

"Madison's right!" Griffin said. "That guy is always telling people that his stories are true, but nobody believes him! If he writes a book about what happened to us, you can guarantee no one will ever think it's real. That way, Madison and I can tell all of our friends, and nobody will believe us, either!"

"Which means we can go home!" I said.

The man looked very serious for a moment, and then a wide smile stretched across his face.

"That's an excellent idea!" he said, snapping his fingers. "If we tell people the truth, they'll think it's so crazy that there's no way they would believe it!"

"Truth is stranger than fiction, that's what my dad always says," Griffin said. Then, he dug into his pocket and pulled out the spare morsel of fruit. "Can we at least keep these?" he asked.

"Ah, the anti-gravity berries," the man said, and he plucked the fruit from Griffin's hand. "Another mystery of the inner world. Yes, I guess you can keep it. They don't work anywhere else except within the new world."

"Really?" Griffin said. He sounded disappointed.

"Correct," the man said. "Oh, they would be quite useful if they did. But unfortunately, no. The anti-gravity berries are yet another one of the many mysteries that SOCRATES hopes to solve."

I pulled the berry from my pocket and looked at it. "Bummer," I said as I popped it into my mouth and started chewing. "It would have been great for Show and Tell at school."

And so, our bizarre experience beneath the surface of the Earth had a happy ending, after all. The man, whose name we never got, told us more about the operation beneath the waterpark, how we'd gotten only a glimpse of what was a huge operation with dozens of rooms, laboratories, and hallways. Even to this day, it seems unbelievable, but it's true. I was there.

Later, after we'd said good-bye to the man, Griffin and I took a shuttle van back to the hotel. My brother was still playing a video game and didn't seem to care that I'd been gone a couple of hours. Mom and Dad came back, all happy and bright, and they showed us a bunch of pictures that they'd taken. I told them everything that had happened that day . . . the absolute truth. Of course, they didn't believe me, but they thought it was a good story, anyway.

We went out to eat that evening, and the next day, we went to the grand opening of the waterpark. It seemed like there were a billion people there! All the while, I kept smiling, thinking that everyone was having a great time on the rides and in the pools, without a clue that a strange new world was right beneath them, hidden in the ground.

I found Griffin, and we hung out for the

afternoon and throughout the remainder of the weekend. The waterpark didn't seem so spooky during the day, but I was uneasy all afternoon, and even a bit frightened. I knew what was in the ground beneath the park, and I found myself looking into the crowds of splashing kids and adults, wondering if, perhaps, one of the creatures from the underworld had found their way out. I was jittery, and whenever someone moved quickly or surprised me, I jumped. And that's the reason that, to this day, I stay away from all waterparks. All of them remind me of the nightmare I experienced beneath WonderSplash. I knew I was never going to forget what we'd experienced the day before. I also knew that there was no one else on Earth who'd had a horrifying experience like we'd had.

Boy, was I wrong about that.

I spent a couple of weeks compiling a bunch of notes, detailing the experience Griffin and I'd had at the waterpark. Then, I mailed everything to that author with the weird glasses. I didn't know if he would turn our story into a book, but you never know. Writers are kind of weird when it comes to stuff like that.

In August, we spent almost a month at our relatives' home in Utah. My cousin, Tony, told me all about an experience he had with zombies, and he described it in such detail that I had to believe him. So, I told him all about what happened to us at the waterpark, knowing that he wouldn't believe a word. He says he believed me, but I don't think he did. And I wasn't worried about him telling anyone else, because I knew no one would believe him.

School started in the fall. I like school, and I'd been looking forward to it. I would see all of my old friends and meet new ones.

And I got a new teacher. His name was Mr. McGillan, and he had just moved to Wyoming from Alabama. He talked sort of funny, with an odd southern accent, which I thought was actually kind of cool. He was nice, and I liked him right away.

But I also liked him because on the very first day, instead of telling us what we were going to learn and what we were going to do, he told us to put away our pencils and papers.

"What each one of us is going to do," he said, "is tell the class about the strangest thing that happened to you over the summer."

That was fun! Lots of kids had some pretty strange and scary things to relate. Nothing, of course, came close to the experience Griffin and I'd had at the waterpark.

But that's not the story I told, because I knew that no one would believe me. They would all think I had gone crazy! Instead, I told the class about how I had been freaked out by a racoon that had gotten stuck in our garbage can next to our garage. Everyone had a good laugh.

Finally, after all of my classmates were done speaking, one of my classmates raised his hand.

"Kyle, you have a question or something to add?" Mr. McGillan asked.

"What about you, Mr. McGillan?" Kyle replied. "What was the strangest thing that happened to you?"

Mr. McGillan had been seated behind his desk. He stood and walked around it, stopping in front of the entire class.

"That's a good question," he said. "Actually, the strangest thing that happened to me didn't really happen to me. It happened to my nephew, who is probably about as old as most of you. And it didn't happen last summer. It happened a couple of years ago."

He paused, then continued.

"But I don't think any of you would believe it," he said.

I thought about what had happened at the waterpark, then spoke.

"What?" I said. "What happened to your nephew?"

"Let's just say that he barely escaped with his life, and he's lucky to be alive today."

He said those words with such cold seriousness that a dark shadow seemed to fall over the class, giving all of us a chill.

"What was it?" a girl asked quietly.

Mr. McGillan looked at the clock. "I suppose," he said, "I'll have time to tell you my nephew's story before we let out for lunch. But someone tell me: do you have army ants here in Wyoming?"

We all looked at each other. No one seemed to know.

"Well," Mr. McGillan continued, "I suppose it doesn't matter. But there are army ants in

Alabama, and they're the fiercest things on six legs."

"Yeah, but they're only that big," one boy said, raising his thumb and forefinger up for all to see. "They're just itty-bitty things."

Mr. McGillan shook his head. "Not these," he said. "I'm talking about army ants that are as big as you." He pointed directly to me, then pointed to one of my classmates. "And you. And you, and you and you."

Again, a cold chill swept through the class. Mr. McGillan spoke so quietly, so seriously, that we knew he wasn't making up anything.

"What happened?" someone whispered.

Silently, Mr. McGillan walked to his desk and retrieved a tall stool that was next to it. He pulled the stool to the center of the room, and sat.

For a moment, he said nothing. He just sat there, looking around the room. Then, he got up and walked to the door, closed it, and turned off the lights. The only glow in the room came from the two windows on the far side of the classroom.

Mr. McGillan returned to the stool, and

spoke.

"What happened to my nephew is probably the most unbelievable, incredible thing imaginable. And it's true. Every word of it. Oh, I know that while I'm telling the story, most of you won't believe it. But once I get to the end, when you realize what *actually* happened to my nephew and his friend, it will make sense. You'll realize that it really is true . . . and it all started with an innocent hike into the forest."

Mr. McGillan kept talking, relating one of the most bizarre tales I'd ever heard. The whole class hung on his every word, so much so that when the lunch bell rang and Mr. McGillan still hadn't finished, nobody moved. We were mesmerized by what had happened to his nephew, terrified, even, at how giant, angry army ants had ambushed Alabama.

Next:

#39: Angry Army Ants Ambush Alabama

Continue on for a FREE preview!

1

"Bo! Come here, buddy! Want a treat?"

The yellow Labrador looked up from the garbage can he was sniffing and wagged his tail. Seeing me, he began trotting happily in my direction, mouth open, tongue flopping back and forth. Bo knew that I always had a treat for him, and today, it was a little bit of my peanut butter and jelly sandwich that I hadn't eaten for lunch.

"Want to go for a hike in the woods?" I said to the dog as I tossed him the small morsel. Bo gulped it down and followed me as I walked up the driveway, alongside our house, past our white metal storage shed, and into the woods. He stopped to sniff the corner of the shed, but quickly caught up to me.

Although he's not my dog, Bo and I have been friends for several months. He's a stray, and I don't know where he lives. Probably in the woods. He has no collar and he's kind of dirty, but he's very friendly. Although there are only a few houses near ours, most of the people who know the dog are nice to him. I've tried to get Mom and Dad to let me keep him, but they keep telling me no.

And they also don't like it when I feed him, because they say it keeps him coming around. So, I have to be a little sneaky when I give him treats. I really wish I could keep him. I think it would be cool to have a dog to keep me company all the time. In fact, I'm the one who gave him his name.

My name is Scott McGillan, but everyone calls me Scooter. I live near Russellville, Alabama. It's not a big city, and me, Mom, Dad, and my younger sister, Elise, live on the outskirts of town, where there are lots of woods and a few swamps. We moved here from Birmingham, Alabama a few years ago, when Dad took a job working for computer software company. The place where he works is only about a mile away from our house, through the woods. It's a huge building surrounded by a tall mesh fence. I've hiked back to it a bunch of times. Dad, however, has to drive, and the road is winding and curvy, so it takes him about ten minutes to get there.

And I like where we live now. I liked Birmingham just fine, because I had a lot of friends that lived nearby. Here, the only friends that live close are Connor Perry and Annie Shepherd.

But the big difference between where we used to live in Birmingham and where we live now near Russellville is the forest and swamps. I love hiking in the woods, exploring, climbing trees, and catching toads, frogs, and turtles.

With Bo at my heels, I traipsed through the forest, sweeping branches and limbs away from my face. The only trails in the woods were the ones I made, and I knew the forest like the back of my hand. I've spent a lot of time back in the woods, and I've never gotten lost.

Today, I was headed to my favorite climbing tree. I'm not sure what kind of a tree it is, but it has lots of branches and I can climb almost to the very top.

"I need to teach you to climb trees, Bo," I said, as I patted his head. "You'd be famous."

When I reach the tree, I grabbed the lowest branch with both hands and swung myself up. Bo stopped and looked up at me. Then, he wandered off, sniffing the ground, searching whatever it is that dogs search for.

Now, before I go any further, you need to know one thing: I'm a good tree climber. I'm careful, I'm not afraid of heights, and I can climb just about any tree.

So, as I was groping branches and pulling myself up through the tree, I was surprised to hear a loud snap, and even more surprised to find a dead branch in my hand that had broken from the trunk.

In a flash of hot panic, I quickly dropped it and reached up to try to grab another branch, but it was too late. I had lost my balance. My foot slipped off the branch beneath me, and I tumbled backwards, knowing all too well that I was in deep trouble.

If I would've fallen to the ground, I would've broken a leg, and arm, or my back. Maybe all three.

But I got lucky.

I had only fallen about a foot when I slammed into another branch. It broke my fall, knocking me sideways. Almost by accident, my arm looped around another branch, and I was able to grab hold, stopping me from tumbling any farther. I froze, gripping the branch, catching my breath. My heart was racing. Twenty feet below, Bo let out a bark. I looked down to see him looking back up at me, wagging his tail anxiously.

"I'm okay, buddy," I said.

Carefully, I began making my way down the tree. I was extra cautious, making certain that the branches I was grabbing onto weren't dead.

Bo was waiting for me with his front paws on the trunk. When I dropped to the ground, he licked my hand and wagged his tail like crazy.

I smiled and patted his head. "I'm fine," I said. "Just a little slip. Sure could've been a lot worse."

I looked up into the tree and once again realized how very lucky I was. I had been quite a ways up. Had I fallen, I could've broken more than my back, legs, or arms. I could've broken my neck.

Several feet away, on the ground, was the branch that had broken off. Instantly, I noticed there were things on it that were moving .

Taking a couple of steps closer, leaning down, I suddenly realized what they were.

Ants. Hundreds of them. Maybe thousands.

They were pouring out from inside the dead branch.

"Sorry about wrecking your home," I said. Bo looked at me and cocked his head, as if I was speaking to him.

"No, Bo," I said to the dog. "I'm talking to the ants."

Again, I looked at the branch, at the hundreds of ants scurrying all over it, pouring out onto the ground and scurrying up-and-down blades of grass and other small sticks. I marveled at how fast they moved. When I was in first grade, I had an ant farm. It was like a very thin, plastic aquarium filled with white sand. It was fascinating to watch the ants build tunnels and climb through them.

But that was when I was in first grade. This year, I would be going into sixth grade, and I wasn't all that fascinated by little tiny ants anymore.

But what was about to happen to me had nothing to do with tiny ants. It had everything to do with *giant* ants, ants that were bigger than me, nearly the size of grown adults. Never in my life had I been afraid of insects.

That was about to change.

3

I was getting hungry, so I decided to go home and grab a snack. My friend Connor, who lives about a mile away, had gone to the hardware store with his dad. I hoped that he would be home by now. We always had fun when we got together. Annie Shepherd also lives about a mile away, but in the other direction.

Bo followed me through the woods, but when we reached the white metal shed, he took off on his own. Where he went, I hadn't a clue . . . which is why I worried about him. Sooner or later, I knew something was going to happen to him. I hated to think about that.

Before I got into our house, I heard a familiar voice call out.

"Hey, Scoot!" Connor said, and I turned to see him riding up our driveway on his bicycle.

"Hey, yourself," I said with a wave.

"Is Annie home?" Connor said, as he approached me and stopped, taking his feet off the bike pedals and placing them flat on the pavement. I think secretly, Connor really likes Annie, but he just won't say it.

"I don't know," I said.

Connor looked me up and down. "It looks like you've been rolling around in the woods," he said.

"Worse," I replied. "I fell out of a tree."

"Really?" He asked.

"Yeah, sort of," I said. "I was climbing a tree in the woods when a branch broke. I fell, but another branch broke my fall, and I didn't fall to the ground."

"You're lucky," Connor said.

"You can say that again," I replied. "I was just going to grab a snack and then head out into the woods again. Wanna come?"

"Sure," Connor replied.

I went inside, where Mom was putting on her shoes.

"There you are," she said. "I have to run over to Susan's house to help her with her computer."

"Is Elise staying?" I asked, hoping that my little sister was going with Mom. If she didn't, that would mean that I would have to stay home and babysit her. Elise is only six, so she can't be alone on her own. She's a good kid, but I really didn't want to have to stay home with her.

"She's coming with me," Mom said.

Whew.

"Connor is waiting outside. I was just going to grab a couple of cookies and we were going to go for a hike in the woods."

"Be careful," she said, standing up and

plucking her car keys off the kitchen table.

"I always am, Mom," I said, but there was no way I was going to tell Mom that I almost fell out of a tree.

Outside, I gave Connor two chocolate chip cookies and looked around for Bo. Mom didn't know it, but I brought a chocolate chip cookie for him, too. I didn't see him anywhere, so I just put the cookie out by the mailbox. If Bo happened to wander along, I was sure he'd sniff it out.

While we walked past the side of the house, past the white metal shed, and into the woods, Connor told me all about the fishing trip he had been on with his dad the day before, saying that he'd caught a bunch of catfish. I wasn't into fishing all that much, but Connor loved it. Last year, he skipped a day of school to go fishing on his own, and got into a lot of trouble.

"Where do you want to go today?" Connor asked.

"Let's go back to the big pond and see if we can find any snapping turtles," I said.

"The pond that's close to where your dad

works?" Connor asked

"That's the one," I replied.

"Sounds good," Connor said. "Are there any fish in it?"

I shrugged. "I have no idea," I said. "But I caught a big turtle there last year. I'll bet he's even bigger this year."

I liked Connor a lot. He's much like me: he wasn't all that much into video games, computers, or television. He liked to be outside, having a real adventures, doing real things. Our friend Annie was the same way. She would much rather be outdoors than inside. And she preferred to hang around with us rather than other girls her age.

Soon, we approached the big fence that surrounded the company were my dad worked. In the distance, we could see the sprawling, single-story building. There were a few cars in the parking lot.

Following the fence line, we continued on until the forest opened up to a large field. At the other side of the field was the pond.

But before we got there, Connor found

something.

"Look," he said, pointing. "What's that?"

I looked at where he was pointing and saw a large hole in the ground. It was big: much bigger than what a rabbit or a squirrel would've made. This hole was big enough for me to climb into.

We walked over to it. The unearthed dirt appeared to be fresh, and there were strange tracks all around.

"Is it a bear den?" Connor asked.

"I don't think so," I said, as I knelt down and curiously into the hole. "Dad says that there are black bears around, but they are supposed to be really rare. Not many people see them."

"You're probably right," Connor said. "And those marks in the sand don't look like bear tracks."

I turned my gaze from the hole and looked at the ground. The tracks were nothing like I'd ever seen. The markings were large, bigger than my foot, and look like they could have been made by sharp claws.

Strange.

I stood. "Well, whatever it is, I don't think it's a bear. Maybe it's a big fox or coyote."

"Must be an awfully big fox or coyote," Connor mused.

"I can't think of anything else that would make a hole that size," I said. "I mean, I guess it *could* be a bear, but these tracks don't—"

I stopped speaking when I realized that Connor wasn't paying attention. He was looking up over my shoulder, into the distance. His eyes were growing wider by the second.

I turned to see what he was staring at.

My jaw fell.

My pulse raced.

My temples pounded.

At the edge of the woods, climbing a large oak tree, was an ant . . . but we were easily fifty feet away from it.

How were we able to see an ant from so far away?

Simple: The ant was bigger than I was!

"I have a really, really bad feeling right now," Connor said in a trembling voice.

I had to admit that I had the same feeling. Not only was I freaked out by what I was seeing, but I also somehow knew that this is only the beginning of something that would be far, far worse.

"What . . . what is that thing?" I stammered.

"It's a giant ant," Connor said.

While I had heard about enormous insects

that live in different parts of the world, I'd never heard or seen anything like this. The biggest ant I think I have ever seen was probably no more than a half an inch long.

While we watched, the ant climbed about the tree, crawling up the trunk and out onto a very large branch. It was every bit as nimble as a squirrel. It even crawled beneath the branch and hung upside down for a moment, before climbing right side up.

"I think I know what made this hole and the ground," Connor said.

I managed a quick glance to the ground and looked at the tracks. It wasn't difficult to imagine the strange claw marks being made by the legs of the monstrous insect.

"Remember that book we read in school last year?" I asked. "The one about those giant crickets in Colorado?"

"Yeah," Connor said. "That was bizarre. But that was a book, and it was just a made up story."

"Well," I said, "nobody's making this up. I know what I'm seeing."

"Great," Connor said. "Now that we both know what were looking at, let's get out of here. There's no telling what that thing can do if he sees us. Ants can move pretty fast."

"Okay," I said. "But we've got to tell someone."

"Who?" Connor asked.

"I don't know," I answered. "Maybe the police. Someone's got to know. That thing is probably super dangerous. Follow me. Let's move really slow through the field and hope that thing doesn't see us. When we make it to the woods, we can run."

I was about to take a step when I heard a noise. The day was warm, and a sheen of sweat glistened on my face. Yet, a cold chill fell over my body.

In the corner of my eye, there was movement close by.

Another cold wave of horror washed over me. Connor and I both turned our heads, slowly, looking down.

Several feet away, a large leg appeared from

the hole.

Then another.

We backed away. Connor grabbed my arm and held on in terror as we continued to slowly back step.

Then, an enormous head appeared. It was an ant, but it was wearing some sort of hat, some sort of dark brown beret. In one claw, it appeared to be carrying some sort of radio.

In seconds, the enormous insect was out of the hole, in full view. We watched while it raised up on two legs, standing like a human. It appeared to be looking at the other ant that was in the oak tree on the other side of the field.

Then, it turned and looked directly at us. I will never forget the feeling I had when the insect's eyes met mine. It was a paralyzing moment, and I stopped in my tracks. Connor, still holding my arm, stopped, too.

For the moment, the insect just stared at us. Then, it turned and looked at the other ant in the tree, then turned back to glare at us.

And without any warning, the creature

dropped the radio he was carrying. It fell to the ground and landed near one of his legs. The insect then dropped to all six legs . . . and came at us.

ABOUT THE AUTHOR

Johnathan Rand has been called 'one of the most prolific authors of the century.' He has authored more than 75 books since the year 2000, with well over 4 million copies in print. His series include the incredibly popular **AMERICAN CHILLERS, MICHIGAN CHILLERS, FREDDIE FERNORTNER, FEARLESS FIRST GRADER,** and **THE ADVENTURE CLUB.** He's also co-authored a novel for teens (with Christopher Knight) entitled **PANDEMIA.** When not traveling, Rand lives in northern Michigan with his wife and three dogs. He is also the only author in the world to have a store that sells only his works: **CHILLERMANIA!** is located in Indian River, Michigan and is open year round. Johnathan Rand is not always at the store, but he has been known to drop by frequently. Find out more at:

www.americanchillers.com

All AudioCraft books are proudly printed, bound, and manufactured in the United States of America, utilizing American resources, labor, and materials.

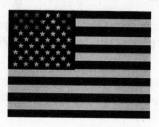

USA